"Brian Hioe's *Taipei at Daybr[...]* [...]
depiction of an alienated you[...]
as he roams from New York t[...] [...] [...]
in the tradition of Camus and Dostoyevsky, this novel makes
its own mark by setting the story against the backdrop of
a pivotal moment in contemporary Taiwanese history. Hioe
is an intelligent and gifted new fictional voice, and *Taipei
at Daybreak* is a critical contribution to multiple literary
lineages."

Shawna Yang Ryan, author of *Green Island*

"An insightful portrait of a Taiwanese American activist
caught between worlds and battling inner turmoil. Set
against the backdrop of transformative protest movements,
it's a sombering tale of identity, purpose, and the power of
media in turbulent times."

**Clarissa Wei, author of *Made in Taiwan: Recipes and
Stories from the Island Nation***

"With so much global interest in Taiwan politics today, Hioe
cuts through the noise in a much-needed way. This story
presents Taiwan through a fictional lens based in real history
that goes far beyond description. Hioe is able to tell the
world about Taiwan, its politics, and its activism, without the
over-romanticism or glamorization of its dire complexities."

**Lev Nachman, co-author of *Taiwan: A Contested
Democracy Under Threat*, Assistant Professor of Political
Science at National Taiwan University.**

"*Taipei at Daybreak* offers a deeply personal reflection on the identities of the Taiwanese, grappling with uncertainty both in the world and within the mind. It explores the rise and decline of social movements with a sharp, unflinching eye on the realities of activism at the forefront of the Sunflower Movement. Brian Hioe intertwines disillusionment with liberalism and a critique of urban capitalism, while also reflecting on the existential search for meaning in a world rife with contradictions. An anarchist account at its most mature, this novel delves into the heart of political struggle with both insight and hope."

Netiwit Chotiphatphaisal, Thai activist

"*Taipei at Daybreak* articulates a groundbreaking genre of activist memoir that is both passionate and devastating. It captures the Taiwanese American diasporic voice from Occupy Wall Street to the Sunflower Movement."

Wen Liu, author of *Feeling Asian American: Racial Flexibility between Assimilation and Oppression*

"Written by one of the most dedicated English-language journalists covering Taiwan, this novel is a startling page-turner that dives into the complexities of political activism and personal desire. Dogged by guilt and desire, the young protagonist is keenly perceptive of the social underdogs during the most drunken hours in New York, Tokyo, and Taipei."

Ta-wei Chi, author of *The Membranes*

Taipei at Daybreak

Taipei at Daybreak

Brian Hioe

Published by Repeater Books

An imprint of Watkins Media Ltd

Unit 11 Shepperton House

89-93 Shepperton Road

London

N1 3DF

United Kingdom

www.repeaterbooks.com

A Repeater Books paperback original 2025

1

Distributed in the United States by Random House, Inc., New York.

Copyright Brian Hioe © 2025

Brian Hioe asserts the moral right to be identified as the author of this work.

ISBN: 9781915672537

Ebook ISBN: 9781915672544

All rights reserved. No part of this publication may be reproduced, stored in a retrieval system, or transmitted, in any form or by any means, electronic, mechanical, photocopying, recording or otherwise, without the prior permission of the publishers.

This book is sold subject to the condition that it shall not, by way of trade or otherwise, be lent, re-sold, hired out or otherwise circulated without the publisher's prior consent in any form of binding or cover other than that in which it is published and without a similar condition including this condition being imposed on the subsequent purchaser.

Printed and bound by CPI Group (UK) Ltd, Croydon, CR0 4YY

Table of Contents

Part 1

In 2013, at twenty-one, I drifted into Taiwan, having already spent many summers there since I was a child. I had spent the previous two years fleeing New York. I'd finished college somehow, graduated, went to Tokyo, came back, and then fled again. When I left for Taiwan, the break seemed permanent. It wasn't that I didn't care about New York. Most likely I would be back someday. Probably my life would be an endless cycle of leaving New York for Asia and Asia for New York. I told my parents that my plan was to work on my Mandarin then apply to graduate school for a degree in Chinese literature. I had no real plans like that.

The first summer in Taipei, I was a wreck. The past year had seen all my hopes, all my expectations for the future, collapse. I had seen Occupy Wall Street come and go; I had lost my best friends, encountered evil face to face, and seen a trace of my own features in it. All that had precipitated a crisis in me, and it didn't seem like anything mattered. I had read a lot about Taiwan's history, but the concerns of the island seemed so small in the grand view of things. I felt that, as a leftist, I should think of the big picture. That meant I shouldn't mind if China swallowed up Taiwan, for instance. The Left stood for the abolition of nation-states and borders, after all; it would be easier to work toward the dissolution of all nation-states if there were fewer to abolish. So I didn't mind the existence of empire if it meant hastening the unification of the world. That was being *rational*, I believed. Taiwan was the "orphan of Asia," and China had said they would reclaim it by 2020. Sometimes I suspected that most of the world believed that this was inevitable.

Would there still be a Taiwanese people in the future? Could I really say I was Taiwanese? Above and beyond the complexities of my diaspora background, I was descended from those that came with the Kuomintang (KMT) to Taiwan, and most members of my family thought of themselves as Chinese. At that point, only 10 percent of the population were descended from people who'd arrived after 1945. That 10 percent came to constitute a privileged economic and political elite during the martial law period, a colonial ruling class presiding over those who'd already been there: descendants of earlier waves of Han migrants and indigenous people who had inhabited Taiwan for thousands of years.

Taiwan's martial law period was once the longest in world history. Known as the White Terror, it was the era from which Taiwan's "sadness" originated. But that "sadness" remained a thing unknown to most of the world. Despite having been forced by the democratization movement to relinquish power and permit free elections since the 1990s, the KMT was allowed to exist as a political party, and it continued to run candidates for office. They had retaken power in 2008, with a KMT president and a majority in the legislature.

Even though the KMT had originally come to Taiwan because of its defeat by the Chinese Communist Party during the Civil War, it advocated the unification of Taiwan and China. Perhaps they believed that they would be allowed to get their privileges back if Taiwan became a part of China — many perceived themselves as having lost what they'd once had after democratization. They had tried to rebuild China in microcosm, driven by nostalgia for an imagined past, or perhaps because of the trauma of past revolutions — a way in which the unresolved past continued to haunt the present. That was why all the streets and places were named after locations in China. The Republic of China — the legal name for Taiwan and the name of the KMT's government-in-exile — was a republic of empty signifiers.

The place I'd found myself growing up in was empty too, as close to nowhere as I could imagine, just a desolate speck on the edge of New York City, a place that barely seemed to even deserve a name. In the no-place that was my town, you could always feel the emptiness creeping in on you. It was in the shadows of the alleys, the corpse of an insect in the grass being devoured by other insects, or lingering on the edge of the forest. When we went into the forest as children, we would always find the bodies of animals strewn about by some predator as though the discarded refuse of a meal.

Somehow, the town's emptiness got into me, perhaps in an unguarded moment squatting over the scattered parts of some eviscerated animal among the trees or lying in bed at night with the windows open, half asleep, and in a way it became my companion, *the emptiness*. Looking back, it's hard to know whether it was the town's and my own American emptiness that stole into me, or the emptiness of Taiwan, passed down through the generations. Perhaps they overlapped and intermingled, giving me an emptiness distinctively my own. Either way, in my bed at night or in those shadowed alleys, or out on the fringes of the town, *the emptiness* spoke to me and gave me a creation myth, explaining that the ground I walked on and the buildings I saw, the sky, our flesh, everything in the universe, was just the corpse of something that had come before; that since the Big

Bang, the universe had been a corpse, time an endless succession of corpses, and that I myself was just a maggot feeding on that corpse-universe. Even without having yet seen the world, I had the sense that one day I would have to consume myself or I would consume the world. *The emptiness* told me I would have to die before I devoured the world.

As one of the first Asians in the area, I always stood out. As I grew up, there were more, mostly moving from the city. In school, I always felt a sense of distance from them — they took pride in their grades, mostly hung out with each other, and in many ways, I felt, were embracing stereotypes — while they labeled me as a weirdo who was friends with a lot of white kids, had long hair, played in a band, and was always trying to organize protests. They felt uncomfortable about me because I troubled the distinctions they drew between themselves and others.

By the time I arrived in Taipei, I could barely remember life before activism. I had been involved in politics since I was fifteen, and at some point I had become an organizer, running an activist group during high school; it was then that I had my first taste of leadership, becoming the head of a student group about human rights. We organized fundraisers, rallies, those kinds of things. Each week in our club, we discussed a different country. But the map of the world itself seemed to be just so much desolation, full of blank nations that we knew nothing about other than that terrible things went on there. That was my idea of the world then — place after place full of senseless killing. Death was everywhere, and even maps themselves were originally made from the skins of animal corpses. It just hadn't occurred to me yet that America was also a place like any other — or, for that matter, that Taiwan was as well. It was hard to discuss America as though it were just another nation-state among many. And was Taiwan in fact a nation-state at all? I wasn't sure.

By my first year of college, I had already become bored of a liberal politics based around the sort of humanitarianism that I had embraced in high school, and I fell in with a group of anarchists. To demonstrate against worker lay-offs, we undertook a three-and-a-half-day hunger strike at the end of the fall semester, occupying the lobby of the main building. It was badly planned and didn't win favor. That was the first time I really felt the hate of the campus directed against a small group of people who were willing to just go against majority opinion.

I decided to get out of there, and the following year I moved to New York City and transferred to NYU. And so, when Occupy Wall Street rolled around, I was there from day one. Most of the participants had gotten their information about it from the Internet. The original callout came from a magazine dating back to the anti-Iraq War movement, *Adbusters*. I didn't think it would amount to much. In the beginning, the plan was for individuals to gather, to coalesce into working groups, and then for a single demand to emerge from the general assembly. What this amounted to in practice was sectarianism and identity politics, and massive infighting took place. I wasn't new to these forms of organizing, which were effective when used to coordinate small, tight-knit groups, but as I left the park after observing a long day of inarticulate arguing, I figured it would disperse in time.

Of course, it didn't. Zuccotti Park wasn't the original target of the occupation, but after it became clear on the first day that the police had blocked off the intended route, the march was diverted there. At the time, I lived in Chinatown, in an NYU dorm on the border of the financial district, fifteen minutes' walk from the park. It's a strange feeling to be in the midst of things and to know that the next day you could turn on the TV and watch what was utterly mundane for you broadcast on the news as something significant.

I would experience this feeling many times in subsequent years, but this was my first taste of it. A part of me suspected that I liked the feeling of being talked about, even if it wasn't exactly in positive terms. There are plenty of people who end up in activism because they want the attention. Maybe that was me too. There's a strange chill to catching yourself in the background of the news, even just as a fleeting figure.

Those were the years of occupation-style movements, when it was still possible to organize spontaneous gatherings through social media. This was the origin of the transitory occupations that took place all over the world in those years — in the Middle East, Asia, Eastern Europe. Really it was a convergence enabled by technology, though this isn't generally how it's perceived. Occupy in itself was nothing special, but the fact that it took place in New York City, on Wall Street, meant that it was sanctified in some way, as though it offered the template for the protests that came after.

All occupations have to end. When the eviction began, I was still awake reading, although it was quite late. I joined the crowd gathered outside the park, recognizing a few people from the campus Left at NYU and some I didn't exactly know but had seen during protests. There were a large number of cameras from the media. A helicopter was circling overhead. It was impossible to see what was going on in the park itself, but after a while the police began advancing toward us. Some groups attempted to sit down to avoid arrest, and the police began using pepper spray.

I was lucky; I happened not to get any of it on me, but I could feel my throat choke up. Then it was chaos: running, screaming; attempts to fall back; attempts to hold the line. I don't remember too well what I did in the heat of the moment. You find yourself trying to concentrate, to be as aware of your surroundings as possible to avoid danger, but you can only take in so much. It's a helpless feeling, but at the same time, it all has a dream-like quality. In the years to come, in the other movements I participated in, I would come to know that feeling well.

I don't know what happened to the other groups in the crowd, but I fell in with a protest march, and as it moved uptown, black bloc began kicking over trash cans and smashing the glass in all the newspaper racks we passed. Some began to try to intercede with them, arguing that they were affecting the legitimacy of the movement. Still others began chanting that they were police provocateurs.

The police eventually caught up. They surrounded us on both sides and attempted to hem us in. There were announcements by loudspeaker threatening arrest. I found myself pushing up against the police with the others and was thrown to the ground. The crowd quickly retreated, leaving me behind, but I got up and ran. I spotted some people I knew from NYU and found out that one of our friends had been arrested. I called the Lawyer's Guild hotline to notify them, then went on by myself.

I also found out from Twitter feeds I had been monitoring through the night that another protest had broken out by Union Square. I didn't go that far. It was close to 5am by then. I broke off from the crowd by 10th Street and walked all the way back to Zuccotti Park, joining a new crowd that had formed around it. I tried circling around to get some view of what was going on, but to no avail. So I went back to my Chinatown apartment.

It was nearly 6am by then. I got coffee from the twenty-four-hour deli behind my apartment and found out from a friend on Facebook that there was a general assembly planned for 8am at Foley Park. I figured I would read for a bit, then head there to see what was going on. I fell asleep instead and my thoughts drifted toward you, V, as they always do on the edge of slumber. Sleep is in some way a premonition of death, after all. You were the one who taught me that, weren't you? That everything decays and rots. All occupations have to end. At the end of any dream is wakefulness.

Around the same time that the Occupy Movement was taking place, my oldest friend, David, was also living in New York City. He was studying at the School of Visual Arts. We met on a playground one day in elementary school, and growing up he was the only person I had shared interests with in our hometown. It was not just that we were alienated from suburbia, it was that we perceived a sort of violence to it, and we felt that violence in ourselves as well. The violence that came of being from an empty place, of being empty ourselves and able to move only from one moment of emptiness to another. We were in a succession of rock bands through high school and beyond, and most weekends we went down to New York City to watch films in the IFC.

I called myself a writer; David called himself an artist — a painter. He never seemed one for worldly matters, so he was very much into "Eastern" spirituality. Though he was still in art school, he was talented and was making a name for himself. He had art openings once in a while — pretentious affairs he himself disdained, laden with perfume, noise, theatricality, and a sense of occasion. I attended them. I guess I could enjoy them in a way that he didn't. I was always a little envious of his success, though, his being able to accomplish so much at such a young age, but he was also always losing motivation and never carrying things through. I found it frustrating, and combined with my envy, I could sometimes be cruel to him.

I asked him once why he painted. "I don't know," he said, matter-of-factly. "I just feel that I should. That it's something I'm good at."

He usually gave me these kinds of vague, noncommittal answers. That was another aspect of his personality I found vexing; I suppose he didn't understand my drive to change things in the world. He thought it was pointless, that I was just trying to impose my will. "That's the way the world is," he would say whenever I was angry, and he'd tell me that I spent too much time thinking about things beyond my control, while I in turn accused him of having given up on the world and turned toward cultivating his self as means of escape. Apart from the fact that he was white and I wasn't, this was the main difference between us. He had tried to fill his emptiness, to escape his own inner violence with art. As for me, I didn't make anything — I couldn't. And while he seemed to be happy curling into himself and going round in circles, I always wanted to be on the path to somewhere else. He would lose interest and move on to new projects, while I kept at the same interests for a long period of time and never moved on. We had both done some organizing in high school, but I had kept it up and he hadn't; he'd become interested in Daoism, various Eastern philosophies, and meditation.

I had always found David's fascination with Asian culture uncomfortable, and I liked to snipe by claiming that he knew very little about historical Buddhism or Daoism, that what he was interested in was just a form of fantasy on his part — that he saw what he wanted to see rather than what was really there. He always seemed to be dating Asian women, which felt a bit strange to me, particularly as his oldest friend. Sometimes he got fed up with me making sarcastic comments all the time, and I knew I was often just being cruel to a close friend in a way that wasn't productive. Was it that I felt a need to fight with him out of some sense of authenticity? When I got nasty, sometimes I made reference to the fact that I could read some of the texts he was so fascinated by in the original language. It wasn't that I understood them, necessarily, but I could at least read the characters, and he couldn't. It's hard to deny that between the two of us I was the less healthy. David was laid back, while I grew more and more neurotic by the day. I frequently lashed out at people around me, but I knew I was often just acting out my own anxieties.

It was at an opening of his, featuring a series of paintings of circles that he had been making since back in high school, that I met Aoi. The concept behind the paintings was that none were exactly the same, even if they were traced from each other over and over. I joked once that the paintings seemed to capture something of his character, and he had responded that I was like a straight line or an arrow. I was gazing at one of the circles when David spotted me and called me over. "Aoi, this is who I was talking about," he said. "My close friend. Q.Q."

That was the name I went by in those days, Q.Q. My initials. Clearly, I had come up in conversation before. She was wearing a low-cut green dress with her hair tied back. Though she sometimes wore glasses, she hadn't that day. I found her quite beautiful. She looked bored. I came to realize that was a constant for her.

We started hanging out — we had something in common and knew it quickly. I got food with David and Aoi pretty often. Neither of them drank, so it was always just them eating and me eating and drinking. We ate at an Indian place once. There were four Indian places in a single building, and four Indian guys stood outside trying to convince people that their restaurant was a better choice than the other three.

"Did you know," I said once we were seated inside, "it's rumored that all four of these places share the same kitchen?"

"How do you know?" asked David.

"I read it in some guide to New York when I first moved here," I said. "*The Scenester's Guide to New York* or something like that." I laughed. "That was the actual title."

"I wouldn't be surprised," said Aoi.

"Got to make a living, right? It's like Coca-Cola and Pepsi. Everything is the same, just the brands are different."

"That's capitalism, right?" said David. But I knew he was skeptical. David was always a bit weirded out by my left-wing beliefs. He probably thought it was hypocritical for me to be such a critic of his spiritual beliefs while I myself clung to as extreme a philosophy: one that called for the overthrow of everything existing.

"Maybe it's spiritual hollowness," I said. "Everything is interchangeable and replaceable. Even people."

Aoi laughed. She had picked up on the tension between me and David. She once said to me that she thought it was funny. After all, David was white, but he was into Eastern spirituality. I was Asian, but wasn't Karl Marx a white man? I had no great response to that.

After dinner, we went and watched a midnight showing of *Eraserhead* in the IFC. Aoi hadn't seen the film, but David and I had both watched it in high school.

"What did you think?" I asked Aoi after the film finished and the lights came on. Some members of the audience still lingered in the theater.

"I liked it… but I don't think I understood it."

"I don't think there's anything to understand," I said, chuckling. "They take some getting used to, David Lynch films." I looked at David. "What did you think the first time you saw it?"

"I don't think I thought anything."

"But you thought it was a good film. Okay." I laughed. "What was your favorite scene?"

"I liked when his head pops off and you see the baby head," I said. I was fond of the thought that inside of us, we were all just babies, really. The oldest and truest part of ourselves.

"I liked that, too."

"I liked when they made his head into a pencil eraser," said Aoi.

"I also liked that."

"It's like… art," said Aoi. "Making something out of yourself. It was so sweet!"

Sometimes I wasn't sure what reality Aoi lived in. It certainly wasn't the same one that David and I did. I remember one time she suggested that she would be willing to do something like Marina Abramovich's *Rhythm 0*, a conceptual art piece in which the artist stood still in a gallery for six hours, inviting the audience to use the objects she had laid out on a table on her in any way they chose. It led at one point to a spectator holding a loaded gun to Abramovich's head.

"You think you wouldn't end up, like, killed?" I asked.

"Yeah. I think I'd come out okay. You're just too negative about other people"

Another time she suggested that she'd be willing to eat humans if she had the opportunity. "We eat animals, don't we? Humans are animals."

"Sure. But where would you find somewhere they still eat humans? If there's anywhere they still eat humans, how can you be sure they wouldn't eat you?"

"Who knows? Maybe they treat the humans they eat as livestock rather than people. That's what they do in places they eat dogs; they're livestock, not pets," she said.

I always found it a bit surprising how different her art was from David's. She did some designing to earn money, but she mostly thought of herself as a performance artist; her art was about the transient embodied experience of a passing moment, while David had always been a painter from an early age and never really seemed interested in any other medium. He has an urge for something cosmic and transcendent, I suppose, despite all his interest in Eastern philosophy — it was the painting on the wall that would last, while bodily experience would remain confined to the moment it occurred. As for me, I was trying to capture experience in words with my writing — I wasn't sure where that placed me: Was I looking for immortality too, or was it a means to try to capture some deeper understanding of myself in the here and now?

One of her performances — one that clearly took inspiration from Abramovich — really stuck with me. It involved having someone throw objects at her while she guessed what they were when they hit the back of her head. These ranged from a pan to a tennis ball, a monitor, random everyday objects like coins or a set of keys, and even a kitchen knife at one point (though it wasn't sharpened). The end product was a video artwork of the objects being thrown at her while she listed possibilities of what they were. She came out not too much the worse for wear, except for some minor bleeding. Though the performance had made me nervous, the end product was actually a bit comical given the randomness of the objects and the fact that most of her guesses were very wrong. But I found it quite existential somehow — I mean, isn't that the unpredictability of life? Life as more than a closed circuit. Even among a limited, select set of objects, there is still the possibility of error. Was that the origin of what we refer to as "life" in shorthand? I also wondered if what we called hope was just the desperate, misguided belief that there could be something outside of that preordained set of choices.

"You should write a review," she had joked when I said this to her. "Turn it into words." But language was the same game of choice among a closed set of possibilities.

"You always have a lot to talk about in museums," Aoi said to me one day in the Museum of Modern Art.

"That's because museums are full of dead things," I said. "Dead things are all I know about, really." The place that all the mummified, deceased things of the past went when they no longer mattered as possibilities out there in the world.

"What do you think there is after death?" asked Aoi.

"Nothing probably." I shrugged. "I'll find out when I'm dead. Maybe they'll put me in a museum."

"Does it bother you?"

"The thought of death? Probably it does. Does it bother you?"

"No, I don't think so. If there wasn't death, life would be… boring?" Aoi smiled. An empty smile. There was nothing on the other side of that smile.

"Sometimes I wonder if it's like a video game and you just start over when it's done." I shrugged. "Why did you take me instead of David today?" I asked.

"I can always learn a lot from you at museums."

David always complained that I was overly preachy at museums about what I'd read, that it was like listening to the audio tour. I chuckled.

"…Or about anything." I tried to look modest, though I knew it was true. David said sometimes that whenever he read anything new, he always had the nagging sense that I had probably read it already.

"You ever try creating something?" asked Aoi, changing the subject.

"Like art?"

"Like whatever."

"No, never," I said. "I don't think I'm the creative type," I lied.

"It's more like you to take things apart to see how they work than to create things."

"But aren't you like that, too?" I asked.

It was her turn to shrug. "I don't think so." She smiled again. I had assumed that Aoi was just a free spirit. I didn't realize until later that she was also empty, and even back then she was already pretty far gone. Perhaps that was what drew us toward each other, the emptiness that we shared.

During high school, David and I were in New York City nearly every week. Any film we wanted to see, or any exhibition that seemed interesting, any show — well, it'd be in New York City. There was a small scene in our town, but there was always much more to do in the city: the place where capital — social or otherwise — accumulated, and it was our ambition and desire for artistic success that drew us to it too. You can't make it big in the suburbs, and neither of us wanted to be a big fish in a small pond, but equally, it's dispiriting when there's so much more competition. I definitely struggled there more than David did. Maybe he just had real talent in a way I didn't. Nonetheless, after living there a while I found I was growing a bit tired of the city and its pretentiousness. I was in the McNally Jackson or some other downtown independent bookstore, maybe the one next to Cooper Union, and the two people beside me — hipsters around my age — were yammering about Heidegger. Perhaps something in the way they talked about it made me feel nothing but contempt, yet later, when I thought about it, I realized that in high school I would have been tremendously excited if two strangers next to me started chatting about Heidegger.

In those years, I had always felt a need to prove myself against those who were older and knew more. Reading more books was one way to catch up. But it didn't do anything for my sense of anxiety. Why was I so intent on proving myself against others? David told me once that I always seemed to be looking for some way to slip citations into everything. "The world exists to be made into a book," I had said to him. The citations were a way to ward off the specter of death.

When I told Aoi about that experience in the bookstore, she laughed, even if her gaze seemed disinterested. "You're taking the city for granted. You can't have a conversation like that anywhere," said Aoi. She laughed. "You're annoyed because they sound just like you," she said.

I knew that I was a show-off about the books I'd read, too, but still that exchange had irked me on some fundamental level — something had changed. We were sitting in one of the many coffee shops around NYU that I frequented in those years. Initially, I had loved all the event flyers you could pick up in coffee shops and the ever-changing posters on the walls advertising shows or exhibitions.

"I know," I shrugged. "I can't stand it though, those people who've done nothing but read. It's all just an intellectual circle-jerk."

"Because you're one of them."

I shrugged again. I couldn't deny that. And maybe that's why I was drawn to her: she didn't just live a life of books. She was pursuing something more embodied, concrete.

Sometimes I felt that my self was just a repository containing all the books I had read.

Perhaps what she got out of her performance was the same kind of immediacy I could only really find in the middle of protests. But later on, I came to wonder if protests weren't simply their own kind of performance too. Or maybe it was that all art was a kind of protest against reality.

I asked her why she had decided to come to New York. She looked surprised that I didn't know better than to ask. "There are things in New York that you could never experience in Tokyo," she said simply. She had a different relationship to New York City, I knew. She was still in love with the place in a way I wasn't.

There were things in Tokyo you couldn't experience in New York either, I assumed, but that was before I lived in Asia and came to know for myself how it was always looking out toward the West. Uneven development, whatever you want to call it. Any exhibition or movie you want to see, eventually it'll end up in New York. Tokyo — not necessarily, despite being the world's largest city.

Still, I was starting to grow contemptuous of all these people going about their lives. So many of them seemed to be convinced that New York was the World City, but I was skeptical.

I voiced this to her one day. "Why is that?" she asked.

"It's a city full of people with pretensions similar to mine," I said.

"So, it's your self-hatred again." She laughed. She was always making fun of me for my negativity. "Also very New York of you. It wasn't like that growing up?"

"There was only David then," I said.

I really did value my relationship with the two of them. Even in the years after, I knew that had been one of the few times I'd felt a sense of intimacy with anyone. It wasn't easy for me to open up. Partly the intimacy arose because we were all students, and we were young. It wasn't just that David and I were drawn to Aoi and she in some way to the both of us; it was that we were all, in our own way, navigating the bleakness of New York City as young adults at the time. There was a richness to the city, with all that it offered in terms of art and culture or experience, and yet simply to survive was a struggle, what with the high rents, many expenses, and decaying infrastructure. That led to a natural sort of camaraderie between us. There's a Chinese proverb about fish drying out on land that try to keep each other moist with their spit — maybe that was us. I miss that bond, even now, in spite of all that happened afterward. Now all I have is you, V.

David and I had always been rivals, in some form. Or perhaps it's better to say that I had always seen him as a rival. Growing up, he always had a lot of friends, and made them easily, because he was talented. He taught himself to paint and sculpt, learned the guitar, made his own podcast and websites. Creating things came very naturally to him. As for me, all I had were my grades and my books. I was good at absorbing and regurgitating knowledge. But I didn't feel as though I could make anything of any worth. I was frequently bothered by the thought that nothing I did would *last*.

It was ironic: between the two of us, I looked better on paper. I had the higher grades, and later on, I was the one that got into an elite university, while he went to city college. When we started playing in bands together, it was probably because my sense of competitiveness compelled me to take up the guitar, too. He was always better than me, even then. He couldn't count for his life, and his playing tended to just speed up and speed up. I would always get into arguments with him about it. Unlike him, I was classically trained — I played the violin and piano. He couldn't read music. Still, he had a dynamism that I lacked.

Things changed a lot after I took up activism. Maybe that was something I did in order to have something he didn't. He wasn't as invested in it all, even if we worked together. I became more aggressive. Maybe it was true that I had always been the more aggressive of the two of us. Or perhaps the more anxious. But I can't help but think that the role I took up in activism changed me in the way that power changes people. That's part of what draws people to it — the will to power. A part of me just craved that sense of recognition I could obtain through activism. That was something I had that David did not.

To be sure, I never saw myself at the head of movements, I lacked the personality for that — I wasn't exactly the charismatic type. I could be a good number two, but if I wasn't cut out to be a leader I could at least be a footnote to some sort of change in society, and I was fine being a supporting cast member. I was aware of my narcissism, to be sure. And I saw it in many of the activists I encountered around Occupy in those days, particularly those who did end up in positions of leadership — usually by being the loudest voice in the room. I just thought there was a way to channel that into something socially meaningful. That was sublimation, right?

I never asked, but I was pretty sure Aoi was sleeping with both of us. She never said what she wanted. Maybe she didn't actually want anything. Ironically, I made them watch *Jules and Jim* with me once at Film Forum, since it was one of my favorite films. The subtext was not lost on anyone. I don't think any of us were really seeking anything lasting, but I decided that David and Aoi were better suited for each other. I had already concluded that happiness was wasted on me. In the end, I was an interloper who had drifted between them. It made me resent him somewhat.

I called him out to a coffee shop on St Mark's. I remember the day was especially cloudy. An awkward meeting on an awkward topic. "Well, you know me better than almost anyone else," I said, after a long time dancing around the topic. "Just be together with Aoi. You're better for her than me."

David was silent. He took a long sip of his coffee. I looked out the window at the few patches of blue visible through the white clouds. Later, I learned that, for Aoi, art involved consuming other people. The emptiness was something she embraced. As for me? I was fine dying alone; I didn't need to drag other people into my downward spiral.

"You are just not worth it, and anyway you'll probably be dead soon," *the emptiness* told me.

But I didn't die; not then, anyway. And here is something else that you have taught me, V: that the world isn't just phenomenon and epiphenomenon.

The fruit in the garden of Eden was rotten from the beginning, you tell me: a kernel of rot that corrupted everything around it. Decay is something with no origin or end, that spreads in all directions until it consumes the universe. That rot is what we refer to as history, and we are just so much matter that — for a brief time — comes to have consciousness before returning to a state of rest; aren't we, V? One day, that will be true for everything in the universe.

The next time Aoi went back to Tokyo, David went with her.

I wished them well. Then I realized something had gone wrong. They'd dropped off the map, and none of our mutual friends, or even David's family, had heard from them. David's relationship with his family was bad enough that they didn't want to bother searching for them, and so I went to Japan to look for them myself. I knew the kind of people that David and Aoi were, after all. I knew their tastes, their habits, their mannerisms, all too well. Only I stood a real chance of finding them, I thought. I realized that if they really didn't want to be found, they wouldn't be, but it was becoming harder and harder even then to just disappear. I owed it to them to at least look. Besides, I would never have been able to forgive myself if something had happened to them and I hadn't tried to prevent it.

That was what I told myself, but perhaps I was just using it as an excuse to go somewhere else too. Intimacies were often mixed up with a sense of resentment for me. I often suspected that emotional attachments were simply a pretext for doing something else entirely. Maybe that was why I had grown disillusioned with liberal politics: the desire for power and status seemed all too transparent — any authentic politics, for me, had to include an element of self-annihilation. Perhaps that's where the resentment came from too; perhaps I was envious of those who simply pursued what they wanted and needed without having to disguise it. It made me suspect that I wasn't capable of anything like real love — love was always just the way I had to disguise my desires from myself, or another form of obliterating myself.

Dynamics between people shift — you know what the result will be, it's only a matter of time. The whole universe, after all, was just a chemical equation in the process of working itself out until it ended in heat death or cold death. Relationships are like that, too, shadowed from the start by the question of how they will die: in fire or in ice; in winter or summer.

One of the advantages of being an American is that it isn't that hard to uproot yourself. You can always find a job teaching English or something like that. To be sure, it was a strike against me that I had an Asian face, but I did have an American accent. It was ironic, since English was not actually my first language, but it had long since become my dominant one, and so I managed to get to Japan as a language student who taught English on the side. The process would have been simpler had I been a white person, I'm sure.

Navigating the streets in Tokyo was very different from moving around in New York. For one, it wasn't as though I could get everywhere on foot, and I often couldn't read the signs, in spite of how prominent English was. It was hard to negotiate the subway lines radiating out from the heart of the city. Maps were everywhere on the roadsides, but I was still always lost.

I was staying in a dormitory near Nerima, not far from the center of Tokyo. The other residents were mostly students, some international, or young company workers. There was room for socializing, but I mostly kept to myself. I even took showers in the dead of night, mostly for the sake of avoiding interactions. Maybe it was because I felt that I had nothing in common with them and never would — young people who seemed, on the whole, to be fine with lives of capitalist bleakness, living in their tiny coffins, socializing with those who lived in the same dormitory, and then going to sleep to continue the cycle the next day. Perhaps it was simply that I never took the time to get to know them?

It was all too easy to isolate oneself in Tokyo. You could quite easily go a prolonged period of time without any social interactions. A part of me enjoyed the solitude since it allowed me to focus on the search. The neighborhood I lived in was small but charming, a quiet commuter suburb where there were lots of places to eat on the cheap. Breakfast usually meant sitting alone at a donburi place near the station. Lunch might involve eating on my own in the cafeteria at the school I was studying at, and dinner might be gyoza on the way back, at an eatery full of office workers in suits. It was quite a contrast to New York, where eating out was always an expensive social pursuit.

There was much about the city I enjoyed, and often sections of the city reminded me of Taipei. I saw *Onna*, which I had always thought looked uncannily like Aoi, in the National Museum of Modern Art. I saw *Mural on Red Indian Ground* when a Jackson Pollack retrospective passed through. I saw a Gutai retrospective. The circles reminded me of David's work. No circle was ever the same. But it made me afraid — of being trapped in a bad infinity and that everything was just a re-combination of what had come before,. That really there was no abstract and concrete, no progress or regress, just a hollowness without end.

At the same time, it felt like living in a pressure cooker. Day in and day out, squeezing into the packed trains full of tired, often drunk salarymen. There was a desolation in the hearts and minds of the residents — especially the young people — and it began to wear on me. People were never sure if I was

Japanese or not. Sometimes I was stared at on the train by someone trying to pin me. That had always been how it was. In Taiwan, America, or anywhere, I was obviously East Asian, but my features were vague enough that it was not easy to determine which ethnicity I was. That was useful sometimes.

Some months into my stay, the anti-nuclear movement kicked into high gear. Small protests that had previously just involved hundreds suddenly escalated. It was only a year after the earthquake and tsunami that had hit Tohoku in 2011 — "311," as it was known — yet the protests were an alien sight to me; tens of thousands doing little but lining up around the capitol building. Was this a revolution? The "Hydrangea Revolution?"

It certainly made for a strange translation and I was surprised when at the end of the day the crowd just dissipated. There wasn't a desire to stay and expand on the occupation — even when the rhetoric of the movement was presented in terms of life and death. After all, the earthquake, tsunami, and nuclear meltdown that followed had killed thousands and displaced tens of thousands more. Worse, the government response was plagued by mismanagement, and they remained committed to nuclear energy despite fears that the frequent seismic activity in Japan could lead to more such disasters. The nuclear lobby was in bed with the political leadership. I hate the assumption that other countries' politics can only be understood with reference to America, but it was to some extent a "9/11 moment." And yet, despite the largest protests since the 1960s, society didn't change. Perhaps there simply wasn't enough rage in the Japanese public as a whole.

But that didn't mean that there wasn't *any* rage.

I started hanging out at an anarchist bar located in the gay district, all red and black, the clientele anti-fa, Zapatista, and Zengakuren, and where I would talk to the regulars and, when there was a protest, head out with them. I realized then that those were the only sort of people I felt comfortable around — people who on some level felt the same kind of deep anger toward all things that I did. It was surprising meeting someone from the old Zengakuren or Doro-Chiba, groups I had read about but never encountered in the flesh, and which were infamous for their history of violence. The Zengakuren was among the best-known student groups from the 1960s, while the Doro-Chiba traced its descent to a rail union that had infamously tied the president of the rail company to the tracks and run him down in 1949. And yet, talking to them, they all seemed like harmless, overly polite old people. Was this merely what age did to people? Or had they always been like that?

Some protests were small, just a group of people outside of a subway station with a megaphone, shouting to pedestrians that largely ignored them. Was this really how society would change? The tiny left-wing groups I encountered in New York City often liked to claim that any change always began with a fragment of society, but I wasn't convinced that the sheer willpower of some tiny insignificant fragment alone could do it. Or that having the right ideas would cause a fragment to automatically rise to a place of significance in world history. The ratio of police to demonstrators always surprised me, too. It wasn't uncommon for there to be as many police as protesters. They would keep a close eye on demonstrations when they moved through the city, even if it was just a bunch of college students. I knew of raids that had taken place of dormitories of student anarchists, with police mobilizing dozens of officers for places that had just three bedrooms.

It was security theater; an attempt to pacify through a show of force that went back to the student radicalism the 1960s and '70s, and I wondered whether much of contemporary Japanese society could be read as a reaction to that period or if it just indicated how deeply rooted depoliticization had become in Japan. Sometimes it struck me that all society was just a vast security theater, a performance that involves every member. And perhaps I, too, was simply playing my allotted role — though it was hard to say who it was that had given me that role. God? History? Who knew?

I could have done much more in Japan to try to influence how things played out with the movement. But Occupy having only been a year prior, I was maybe still too burnt out, and besides, my language skills were not up to par. I also didn't realize how extraordinary were the series of events I had been living through. After blundering into Occupy Wall Street, I had imagined that social movements were something that would drop into my lap everywhere I went in life. I missed out on a lot of big events because of being blasé. That's something I still regret, but of course protest movements weren't the main reason I was there.

Tracking someone down in one of the world's largest cities wasn't easy, but we had mutual friends who gave me some hints. I checked out places I thought they might have gone to in between my attempts to explore the city, visiting various bars or shops, places that were subcultural, mostly guided by my sense of Aoi's tastes when it came down to it. She was the local, after all, and David tended not to have a lot of strong opinions about what he liked or disliked.

I considered giving up many times. Sometimes I felt guilty, that I should be putting more energy into the search. But there was only so much I could do. It was possible, after all, that they had gone elsewhere. But it turned out to be more a matter of waiting than anything else — waiting and being in the right place. The odds of finding them by mere chance in a city so large were astronomically low. If they preferred not to be found, I just wouldn't find them. If they decided to reveal themselves, they would.

Finally, after half a year in Japan, I tracked down David through a hint from one of those mutual friends. He was living in Takadanobaba — alone.

We met in a small noodle bar. He had a worn look about him and had grown a beard, but he otherwise seemed alright.

"You look like you've gone through hell," I joked when I saw him.

He laughed wearily. "I've been through a lot."

"Mind sharing?"

"I'm still trying to work my way through all of it."

I shrugged. "You don't have to tell me if you don't want to. So long as you can work your way through it on your own."

"It's fine," said David, after a moment. "There's nobody else for me to talk about it with, anyway."

True enough. I remained silent for a while.

"So. What are you doing in Tokyo?" he asked at last.

I took a sip of the beer I had ordered. "Ostensibly, I'm here on an exchange program. The truth is I came looking for you. And Aoi. I came looking for you both."

David nodded. "I'm touched," he said, somewhat humorously. "But thanks." He let out a breath. "Let me tell you, it wasn't easy."

"Oh?"

"Even someone like me, I could have been pulled in, had I been just a little bit weaker."

"I see," I said, hiding my surprise. I laid my palms flat on the table. "I'm sure it's a long story. So. Tell me." I could feel a foreboding. Did I want to know? Would it be something that I later came to regret knowing?

Aoi, it transpired, had at one point joined Aum Shinrikyo, the famed religious cult known for the sarin gas attacks conducted in the mid-1990s — another moment after the turbulence of the 1960s that had perhaps contributed to the apparent terror of public gatherings or political organizations within Japan. She had been involved with Aum's successor organization, Aleph and was a member, a former member, or an affiliate in some way — it was never exactly clear to me which. This had all taken place before any of us had met her in New York, back when she was in Japan. But she had stayed in touch with them.

I hadn't known the exact details, though I was aware that she'd been part of some religious group, and she had spoken of their attempts to brainwash her as though it were just one among the many strange experiences she'd had; she'd managed to understand what they were trying to do to her and got out. It hadn't occurred to me that it could be Aum — a household name in the wake of the gas attacks. For some reason she had decided to subject David to the same experiences. Why? Was she testing him? David had survived, but what if he had broken? Was it that she didn't care? Was she filled with the desire to destroy?

Though David had managed to get out, Aoi had abandoned him, and he had instead drifted into one of the splinter organizations, one that had tried to distance itself from the gas attack but within which there were still unrepentant members. I knew that a man named Uemoto had become the leader of Aum after the gas attacks and the arrest of their spiritual leader, Shoko Asahara. Uemoto became known for his defense of Aum, which tried to change its image under his tenure by rebranding as Aleph. The Circle was another group he had formed, itself a splinter from Aleph.

Circles within circles, splits within splits.

David decided to introduce me, rather nonchalantly, almost as an afterthought, knowing that I would find the encounter "interesting." We went out to a nondescript Tokyo suburb for the meeting, a long journey out on the train, traveling into some remote and distant heart of darkness to what looked to be someone's rather large house. I found it to be unusually grassy and full of greenery given the general drabness of the Tokyo metropolis, a secluded villa set deep in a concrete jungle.

Two cops were hanging out by the gate of the building as we approached. They asked us our names. In a fit of bravado, I told them that my name was "John Smith" — a character from my Japanese textbook. I was nervous and had decided to hide that from myself, and perhaps from David too, by doing something absurd.

They didn't really seem to care, and nobody checked my ID, nor did either of them write it down. They just took it in stride. This indicated to me that in some way it was all for show; more security theater of the kind that seemed to be common in Japan. I saw it with the Zengakuren I had met as well — even though they were getting on in years, every year they would stage a protest and flee into the subways pursued by police. It seemed ritualistic to me, like a ceremony to mark the passage of time, or perhaps some form of repetition compulsion.

We went inside, there was a round of introductions, and we sat down and talked. There was no agenda. It seemed to be a social gathering, and I was impressed that David was able to get by with some level of Japanese when he had struggled with memorizing Chinese characters in the past. There were some exchanges between David and the other ex-Aum members that I couldn't understand. Someone nodded at David, and he nodded in return. "He'll meet you," said David. He remained at the table and said he would let me speak with him alone, then they took me aside to a smaller room to meet Uemoto.

It really did have the air of a meeting with a guru. He had close-cropped hair and a sporty vibe to him; he was around fifty but could have passed for a man in his late thirties or early forties.

Uemoto seemed to be rather curious about me and asked me a number of questions about my background — or perhaps he was just good at projecting interest. His English was quite passable, and in the end I talked with him for more than an hour; he told me that as someone who understood both sides, I could be a bridge between the East and the West at a time when the two would potentially come into conflict. He seemed to be referring to the US and China, as well as to my being Taiwanese.

I found what he had to say quite trite, but there was something about the way he spoke that projected charisma. He claimed that Aum's actions were wrong. But did he regret it? He hadn't seemed to at the time, until he was forced out of the organization. He later spent three years in jail for the sarin gas attacks, though the government seemed to take a light touch with him, while Asahara ended up on death row. It was all quite strange for me, how Taiwan had come up in the conversation in this way. Like many Taiwanese adolescents, I had read Urasawa Naoki's manga *20th Century Boys* during one of my summers spent in Taiwan. The cult depicted in *20th Century Boys* was based on Aum, at least in part. It seemed to me as though it was still something like a cult, but not as dangerous. Just a bunch of lonely people who needed a place to gather. And though I was meeting a man that society considered a terrorist, he and all the rest of them appeared quite normal. But maybe every terrorist organization is just that — a collection of normal people who have been brought to extremes. Everyone longs for something beyond everyday life, don't they? For stories beyond mundane, repetitive, humdrum day-by-day existence. In the years to come, I would meet a number of people like that. It doesn't take much to become a terrorist, I've learned, if the conditions are right; and maybe it's the lonely who are drawn to it — to a commitment that surpasses their commitment to the reality principle. Those of us who are political all ask ourselves: Could we kill or die for an idea? Is it just theater? Just acting out a role until it becomes real suddenly? Is there no other way of synthesizing the grand and universal with the mediocrity of fleshy existence? But there's surely some threshold after which there's no going back, after which we can only wade deeper and deeper, even if it's just into more and more death. Perhaps it's all just one form of theater in response to another; a grand performance composed of other performances. Maybe that's what human history is: minor interlocking performances all the way down. Or maybe it's life itself; underneath it all, and shining darkly through the paper-thin stage sets, there's just *the emptiness*.

Why would Aoi join Aleph? She wasn't a monster as such, just an ordinary person with an ordinary person's fascination with the monstrous, one who strayed too far. It turned out that she had in fact found herself seeking them out after reading an oral history of the organization by Haruki Murakami. Perhaps she was simply bored of life and sought out what was interesting. What could be more interesting than that which society rejects? Than those cast out of a boring society? Maybe, for her, in the end, she couldn't conceive of freedom as distinct from power, and maybe this was the only way she could relate to people. I was used to thinking of myself as different from other people, extraordinary even. But did that mean I was ordinary? Or were the ordinary the ones who were, in fact, dangerous?

"I don't feel free," I remember saying to her once. We were in the financial district. sitting in the shadow of some giant mass of glass and steel that was still under construction. It was the early evening, and we were eating Vietnamese sandwiches I had bought from the eatery across from my dorm in Chinatown.

"Can't you do anything about it?"

"Don't know."

Aoi smiled. Mockingly, I thought. "I don't know about you," she said, "but I am free."

Was I really all that different from her? There was a reason I was always drifting between various social movements. It wasn't necessarily that I cared for the world so much as that I was seeking something to do because I was bored — seeking something interesting that could make me feel genuinely alive. Maybe I was just a thrill-seeker who used politics as a cover for his drive to experience intensities, pain, violence, panic; after all, *the emptiness* was inside of me, too, small but growing, and Aoi was just someone else seeking a way to fill her inner sense void, drifting between episodes in her life, David and I just characters in one of those episodes, just as the two of them were characters in an episode of mine. We were all just background scenery in each other's lives. That's why she had pulled David into Aleph. Because in some ways he wasn't real for her and it would have been interesting to see how he reacted, to see what made him tick, in the process of his being broken down and disaggregated. I was quite manipulative, too, when it came down to it; I too enjoyed pulling things apart and being pulled apart myself, but I was still capable of regret.

You will become like her too, one day, *the emptiness* said to me.

Uemoto smiled an ambiguous smile almost as though he could read my thoughts or see something in me that as of yet

I could not. It seemed our conversation was over. Well, I still had some time left before I turned to ashes — you were my salvation V, that much I still knew.

We emerged from that strange greenhouse-like villa, back out past the police, and began to walk back through the anonymous, maze-like suburbs. Even though the evening had passed without incident, I found I was strangely disturbed. I felt a sense of disquiet. It was hard to focus.

"You're going to stay?" I asked.

David nodded. "I can't exactly go back to my parents. And I still want to find Aoi."

I took a deep breath. "You're not going to give it up? She abandoned you, you know?"

"Yeah," said David. "But I can't hold any grudges against her. If I hadn't gone through that, I wouldn't be the 'me' sitting in front of you here today."

A silence fell between us, leaving nothing but the low, grey concrete walls and secretive hush of the outskirts. The sense stole over me that I was on fire. I was an explosion waiting to happen. I could be but a minor flame in the age of the atom bomb, but still I was a man aflame. Amid the static in my brain, I tried to concentrate on the moment. On the sense of being embodied in the then and there. And yet I felt my thoughts turning back to you, V.

"You want to talk about it?" I asked.

He shrugged and smiled, somewhat bashfully. "Maybe someday. I just realize that it's very easy for certain spiritual practices to be used to convince you of something. Breathing practices. Yoga. Meditation. Those kinds of things. Things that involve bodily experience."

I would burn. I would turn to ashes. This was contingency rushing towards its end. But in the meantime, I would set the world ablaze.

"That by 'discarding the self, the true self will emerge'... Is that what it was?" I asked. This was a line that had stuck with me from one of Murakami's interviewees in his book.

We were all flawed, and for that, all existence must perish. It was time to die! We had yet to live. We had yet to be born. It was time to become destiny.

He shrugged and didn't answer.

"I don't envy you," I said.

"What about you?"

"I have to head back."

"Why?"

I had no answer for him, or even really for myself. What did Nizan say about being twenty? I was twenty years old. Twenty seconds, twenty minutes, twenty hours, twenty days, twenty months, twenty years, twenty decades, twenty centuries — twenty, twenty, twenty-one...! It was the twenty-first century. I had to return to New York. Destiny called. Fate awaited. Why? The time had finally come to sacrifice myself to myself. And suddenly I could feel the flesh rotting within me, the maggots crawling in my brain, the decay weighing on my limbs. All these empty spaces had opened up inside of me, the entrails eaten away. I was both a maggot feasting on the corpse of the universe and a corpse being consumed by maggots from within.

And yet, compared to later, this was a small death — but it was the first time I died, nonetheless.

Part 2

In that summer of 2013 in Taiwan, I fell in with a group of kids who'd graduated high school in the US or elsewhere and then taken a year off to learn Chinese, or who had gone to English schools in Taiwan. It was ironic: when I was in college, I mostly hung out with older grad students. Now that I was out of college, I mostly hung out with high schoolers who were, like me, caught between worlds in some way. Doubly ironic, given that I had spent so much of my life sneering at notions of racial identity, was that I found myself around so much diaspora. As a Marxist, I had viewed racial identity and all forms of nationalism as divisive, a distraction from the task of world revolution. But beneath and behind all those layers of identity, who was I?

The side of the city they showed me was composed mostly of bars and nightclubs. They were getting to know the world as adults, which was probably why such places were interesting to them. As for me, I was already an adult, and it made me feel like the city was rather meaningless, a vast array of places full of young people, falling over each other, trying to find themselves.

I had nothing in common with them, of course, apart from being somehow between places. Periodically, I could see that they looked at me as though I were a space alien that had fallen to the earth — someone who had come from a world of his own, with its own rules. When I met someone new, they always seemed to be impressed that I was from New York. New York had that kind of cultural cachet the world over, I suppose. And yet here I was trying to escape it.

In the last weeks of my first semester in Taiwan, after ending up in a bar with some people from school I didn't know well and drinking too much, I took a nasty fall. I don't remember how, but I chipped off half of my front tooth, put a sizable hole in my lip, and stumbled home. The next day, I woke up and found that I had somehow smeared all of my belongings with blood after getting home that night.

I got my lip stitched up and my tooth pulled the next day. The lip would heal, but I felt self-conscious missing a front tooth. For a few weeks, I wore a surgical mask whenever I was out in public. I pretended I had a cold if anyone asked. Eventually, I got a false tooth implanted. It's still there. I imagine that when I'm dead, they'll find it, screwed into my jaw. I see it every time I have to take an X-ray of my skull. It was strange, becoming desensitized to a metallic, artificial bone implanted into my skull.

The day after the surgery I looked at myself in the mirror, all bloodied, sewn up, and bandaged, and sneered at how pathetic I was. But there was something absurd about it too. What was I doing? How had it come to this, that I had managed to damage myself — permanently — here in this place that was no place. I had no sense of momentum or trajectory now, no sense of forward motion, that I was going anywhere with my life. I was just an object coming to rest.

"This is how you are going to die," *the emptiness* said to me. "Like a dog." I heard that in your voice, V. Perhaps that was the first time you spoke to me, or perhaps it was the first time

I understood that it has always been your voice that I hear whispering to me in my darkest moments.

That summer, I lived in a tiny apartment with no windows that was probably around three ping; that is, the size of three tatami mats. Sitting in there, it often felt as though the outside world had ceased to exist or might never have existed; that reality outside my apartment had been only a figment of my imagination, something I had dreamed up to escape the fact that there was no other reality but the room I was in; and I would go outside periodically just to confirm that the outside world existed.

I could never tell whether it was day or night unless I checked the clock, and my perception of time became more and more fragmented. With no window through which to see things like the setting of the sun or the day gradually darkening, I'd find that while it had been bright and sunny what seemed like just a few hours ago, suddenly it would be deep night, and I eventually came completely unstuck from the progression of time as it orients most people's day-to-day routines. The only consistent measure of time for me was the sound of retching I would hear from upstairs every day, which indicated that it was night. Sound travels strangely in a building composed of boxes, making it impossible to determine exactly where the noise came from. All I knew was that someone living somewhere above me sounded as though they were dying.

Three of the walls of my apartment had wallpaper covered with a pattern of angular shapes, while the fourth had a slightly different design that also incorporated circles. I would stare at the wallpaper for hours during bouts of insomnia, and as time went by, the patterns on the wallpaper would begin to change. The previous resident had left hooks up on the wall, which seemed to drift through the shapes rather than being anchored in place, changing in number from time to time.

I rarely saw my neighbors in the apartment complex, which consisted entirely of windowless boxes like mine. They all seemed to be suit-wearing salarymen who gave me disapproving looks since I was clearly not one of them. I felt at the time that living there somehow completed their identities as salarymen.

As it rains almost daily during the summers in Taipei, I could never tell whether I should bring an umbrella from inside my box. I would always have to ask a friend what the weather was like before I went out. A street nearby contained nothing but pet shops full of small animals in cages. I would walk by and stare at them every day. At closing time, the employees would pack all the small dogs and cats into boxes to take them home and I would wonder what it was like being a creature that a greater power could put in a box at any time, though I myself seemed to have become a being who was always packed away when not in use.

I slowly started to think of the whole of human existence in terms of boxes. I lived in a box in an apartment building, itself a collection of boxes, in a city that was a mass of boxes containing others. To go anywhere — like my office if I'd been one of the salarymen I lived among — I would take a subway or bus, traveling in a moving box to get to from Box A (home) to Box B (office). Life was spent in boxes. I had been born in a box, which is to say, a hospital. When I was dead, they would put me in a box, too.

I eventually noticed small droplets of water seeping out of cracks between the floorboards. I thought it was just my imagination at first, that I was losing it. But then the problem got worse, and I realized I genuinely had a flooding issue. A layer of water eventually accumulated on the floor of my box, destroying several of my books. I had noticed months before that they always tore up the floorboards from the apartments when someone moved out. Mold, probably. The city itself was decaying, as was I.

It's common for landlords to divide up apartments into smaller rooms, even when this involves flagrant violations of the building code, and had there been a fire I would certainly have died. People live in coffin-like apartments all over East Asia, whether in Hong Kong, South Korea, China, Japan, or Taiwan. Rising rents are forcing young people into boxes, where they spend their time when not working long hours for meager pay. You could glance out at the Taipei skyline and see which of the office buildings that dominated the landscape were owned by major conglomerates. That seemed to say something about the society we lived in. A nickname for Taiwan among young people — who lacked the opportunities their Boomer parents had, and who would have to give up eating and drinking for fifteen years in order to own a home — was "ghost island." In the months I spent living there, I thought a lot about a line from Kobo Abe's *The Box Man*, a novel about a man living in a cardboard box: "The more you struggle… the more the box is like another layer of outer skin that grows from the body, and the inner arrangement is made more and more complex."

Even if my apartment wasn't much, I lived in quite an upscale part of town, a stone's throw away from the world's only twenty-four-hour bookstore, Eslite, as well as a number of shopping malls and nightclubs. I had always been a night person, but compared to New York, Tokyo, or anywhere, Taipei was the real city that never slept. But a city that never sleeps cannot dream.

The nice thing about Eslite was that they let you sit, browse, and read through books. The thought of a bookstore that never closes is a romantic one. I liked the thought of all the knowledge of the world being there at your fingertips, even if it had a price tag on it. The story always went that celebrities were in the habit of visiting the Eslite Dunnan in the late-night hours so as to avoid the public gaze. The paparazzi would hang out in the Eslite as a result, hoping to snap them and their partners. That said everything about the place, really. Or it might be full of people who had gone out for the night and were waiting for the first train.

It could still be a place of refuge, but it represented a bourgeois fantasy in some sense. Though it called itself a bookstore, Eslite was really a shopping mall dressed up as something more cultured. Each location contained a bookstore, but the lion's share of space went to stores selling clothes, furniture, stationery, and other products. In the 1990s and 2000s, Taipei's newly emergent middle class was craving culture at a time when the economic boom masked a strong sense of social anomie — this seems to be the need that Eslite fulfilled. I much preferred the night market, a cornerstone of Taiwanese society, a place for friends and families to congregate for anything from dinner to late-night snacks. I loved the stalls that stayed open until 3 or 4am, often attracting club kids or other people who stayed out late. There's a term we have in

Chinese, 熱鬧, referring to the sense of being in a crowd — this was what attracted me to spaces like the night market.

I soon got to know the denizens of the night in my neighborhood. There was one man in particular I ran across often. He had a nightly routine of collecting garbage as he wandered around. He would sort through his discoveries while sitting in a park. The first time I ran across him, I saw him pick up a noose-like rope and walk alone for some distance with it. I followed him for a while, fearful he intended to hang himself. Eventually I saw him discard the rope and return home — I realized afterward that this was a regular thing for him. I came to wonder what these nightly excursions did for him — perhaps they were meditations on the self. Or perhaps he was just bored.

Another woman I saw sat on her scooter every night in front of the building where she lived, scrolling through her phone and watching videos. She would talk to herself quietly, then suddenly break out into shouting. This, too, alarmed me before I realized that it was a regular thing. I realized that the mutterings were often about politics — accusing past political figures, such as preceding Taiwanese presidents, of being responsible for the woes she faced. The world she lived in was one where her daily reality intersected all too directly with the grand dramas of national politics. At one point, posters began to appear around the neighborhood alleging that a movie star was responsible for the death of the poster-maker's family. New iterations, new variants would appear, written in distinctive scrawl, some tortured inner monologue spilling out into public space. The night is often the time where one's inner madness becomes externalized, I suspect.

Even in the midst of so much wealth, there were places where the underbelly of urban poverty showed through, and it struck me how the polished veneer of the city masked a great deal of suffering. You didn't see many homeless in Taipei. But you would come across them on the outskirts of the city. You would find their belongings tied together in plastic bags and wrapped in cardboard, with an umbrella to prevent them from getting wet when it rained; strange flower-like bundles of detritus blooming here and there on the streets.

Just as in Japan, the convenience stores in Taiwan were ubiquitous — and they did just about everything. You could even pay your electric bill or receive packages there. They had instant noodles, tea, eggs, microwaveable meals, coffee machines, and more. Some places, you could even get a clean dress shirt if you had stayed out overnight and had to go to work the next day.

Eating the microwaveable meals, I came to realize they all seemed to be based on a small set of basic ingredients, but that there were many permutations of these. You might see the same kind of noodles paired with different sauces or meat, for example. Then this might be spun out into half a dozen products that had the same sauce paired with another kind of meat or another kind of noodle or rice.

There was the illusion of choice when everything was just a variation of something else. Except, without choice, it didn't seem like real food — it felt like eating zombie food or its simulacra; just something that stood in for food and looked like food and tasted like food, but which was not food, neatly lined up on endless shelves under the fluorescent convenience-store light. Sometimes I fantasized about a future in which, say, mapo tofu or curry — two of the cheapest convenience-store dishes — no longer existed and all we had left was the simulacra of them. Just an infinite array of reproducible flavors, any taste you could think of only existing as some chemical concoction, as the echo of a distant past in which such tastes *did* exist. A world in which food was only eaten in order to survive rather than for any pleasure, and in which it was devoid of genuine taste.

The fact that the dominant convenience store chains — 7/11 and Family Mart — had become places where you could go to pay your bills reflected how powerful their owners had become; they could negotiate directly with the government. A common joke was that 7/11 was something like a ministry of government. Yet it was a brutal job for the clerks, who kept the stores running 24/7 and performed roles ranging from barista to bank teller or postal service staff — all on minimum wage. And the chain-run convenience stores were displacing family-run gamadiam — similar to the New York City bodegas — that had previously offered many of the same services. Convenience stores seemed like a condensation of capitalist alienation, with their bright fluorescent lights and cheery music at all hours of the day.

All that is solid seemed to melt into 7/11 sometimes. In the urban landscape, each building comes to resemble the next, and the city itself comes to seem like a landscape composed of the same basic elements, repeated over and over again — the way a video game might automatically generate landscapes from a limited set of building blocks and pre-rendered elements. It made me feel that the city was just a vast landscape of nullity, in which everything was just the flavorless copy of a copy of a copy. A world with no possibility beyond what already existed.

As you could do anything there, I was willing to bet the clerks saw all manner of people with all manner of lifestyles. Though convenience store clerks were normally anonymous and indistinguishable, I came to recognize some by virtue of the fact that they worked the late-night shift. Two twins worked one of the 7/11s near me, and I'd sometimes come across them in other 7/11s in the same area. There was another where all of the workers were heavily tattooed, had many piercings, and seemed to be into heavy metal, playing songs on a small set of speakers which overlapped uncomfortably with the cheery music from the store radio. They seemed to live in the area as well — I would run into them in the local night market or coming out of the building where they lived.

The places I was most attracted to at night were often those where outsiders congregated. There wasn't much in the way of craft beer or cocktail bars in Taipei then, and I started going to two bars on Fuxing South Road. They had the distinction of being dive bars in the upscale part of the city. The first had no name but was usually referred to as "Pub" by its clients and stayed open until the last customer left. As a result, it wasn't unusual for it to be open until 6 or 7am. Sometimes I would pass and see that the regulars were all still in there drinking at noon. The second, which was named "Brother Tseng's place" after the owner, attracted a lot of people that I was pretty sure were gangsters. The first time I walked in, a stranger approached me to chat, noting that he had never seen me before. He indicated a customer sitting at a back table next to a decoration that looked like an upside-down Christmas tree. "See him? He's a member of the Four Seas Gang. But we're all just friends here." There were several places nearby I knew to be hostess clubs; the stretch of road they were on was only about fifteen minutes' walk from the nightclub district. As such, there was bound to be some gang element in the background of all this — even in sanitized, sterile, commercial downtown Taipei. Sometimes you would encounter a customer who seemed to have gotten off of work from a nearby jiudian, or hostess bar, and needed a drink, perhaps from the stress of having to deflect obnoxious and overbearing male clients all night.

Both were dimly lit and strangely decorated affairs. Brother Tseng's place had a karaoke machine and flashing lights, while the nameless bar had a dart machine. Beer was cheap, at just 200 NT for a large bottle. Cocktails were usually rather badly made — the focus was on the beer. Customers could buy and keep hard liquor in bottles there. Despite how run-down it all was, sometimes you would see customers try to show off their wealth that way.

Brother Tseng's place was the older of the two, having been open for over thirty years at that point. I wonder what it felt like to have put so much of one's self into a place and to be involved in the complex relationships that existed between those who had worked there for decades together. That style of bar traces its roots back to the GI bars that sprouted up in Taiwan when it still hosted US bases, and when Taiwan had served as a vacation spot for American soldiers during the Vietnam War. Ironic, then, to visit these places as an American. I mostly kept to myself in Brother Tseng's place, wary of the gangsters that it was claimed came there, and just observed. I was in the habit of reading through the day's news as I drank, or I might just zone out.

I got to know the regulars better at the bar without a name, which had a more even gender balance than Brother Tseng's place, which had mostly male customers. There were a number of outsiders, too. There was a Singaporean woman who was a single mother and who often came to drink after her daughter was asleep; a stray American man who seemed to have few other friends despite having lived in Taiwan for decades; a middle-aged trans woman — irrespective of the fact that the customers tended to be conservative, they all seemed fine with her. The oldest customer was around eighty, a man who frequently wore a cap and had long hair. He seemed to come because he didn't get along with his family. Most days there was a real estate agent who stayed out until dawn almost every night — according to the owner, he spent over 40,000 NT on drinks in a month.

It all seemed a bit exploitative, but the regular customers there appeared to have found a place where they could enjoy some intimacy and familiarity of a kind. A sort of community, a family even. Maybe I was looking for that myself. A lot of my conversations there were about politics. In the district we lived in, the customers slanted heavily "waishengren" — descendants of those who had come to Taiwan with the KMT, as compared to the Indigenous population and those who were "benshengren," descendants of earlier waves of Chinese migrants. Given my pro-independence views, I argued often, invariably with men old enough to be my father or even grandfather. Their views tended to be highly selective, taking the position that China had already become more or less democratic after the free market reforms of the 1980s, never mind how bad things had gotten in the past few years. The fact that I was young, had grown up in the US, and was highly educated — what with my fancy university degree — made them more willing to listen to me.

Sometimes I wondered if it was the sense of distance I felt from my real family that drove me to seek out such spaces. After all, my politics isolated me from them almost totally; an immeasurable gulf existed between us, and we shared so little in terms of values. Still, perhaps a sense of belonging and acceptance was what I sought out through various political groupings or in my relationships with people like David and Aoi. But if my politics was just driven by fundamental sense of loneliness, that seemed to rather undermine my claims to stand for anything on the basis of some ideology or philosophy.

A part of me did wonder, in fact, whether this was the appeal of the place for me. I had, after all, never been able to speak to my parents about politics; they were always dismissive. And I can't deny that part of it might have been the sense of adventure — or danger — of being on even just the periphery of Taipei's dark underbelly.

At the nameless bar, there were two customers that the regulars agreed were in all probability gangsters, and they were accordingly treated with the appropriate caution. I can't confirm this, since gangsters usually don't go up to you and tell you directly that they are gangsters. The pair would show up drunk, demand more to drink, and never pay for anything.

Eventually the owner would have to call a cab to remove them. I remember there was a time that they wanted to go to karaoke and half of the bar felt too afraid to refuse them. Although I had wanted to go for the experience, the other regulars told me to stay — since I was the youngest, they probably felt somewhat protective of me. By the time the two came back, a few hours had passed. They seemed trashed.

From interacting with that duo, I learned that gangsters are strangely socially awkward people. They have no way of interacting with others except through masculine bravado; what they seem to hunger for most of all is to be respected, which means being feared. For them, that's masculinity, I guess. Or perhaps the desire for power — to be feared — is just the result of loneliness.

Why was I so interested in these people? Sympathy for the marginalized, the disprivileged, the oppressed. Probably that's what had attracted me to the Left to begin with. Several years before, I would have scoffed at this. Political commitments forged on the basis of something as weak as emotional attachments were a liability, I had once thought. The Left wasn't just about identification with the most oppressed elements of society. The Left was about the intellectual project of realizing human freedom. That's what I had believed, once. But perhaps I was just a romantic at heart. What was it, after all, that moved people? And yet I was just a visitor, while they lived there. A part of me felt that my gaze was simply that of the voyeur. How pointless.

Still, V, though it came a bit earlier for me, when I look back on it now, that was the year that put us on our differing paths. You and I would have had to face that sooner or later, born as we both were under the shadow of the same arbiter of death.

I still hope that it's you who will be my redemption, that it will be my corpse rather than yours in the abyss of time.

Part of my interest in going to the bars was that it allowed me to speak to people from a different social stratum, to get out of the echo chamber of progressive young people I was otherwise surrounded by — I had been growing disillusioned with how little my classmates got out of their expat bubble. There's a world in Taipei composed of English speakers — either expats, Taiwanese who grew up in English-speaking environments or who spoke it adequately enough, and Taiwanese Americans — that constitutes a kind of parallel reality; there was a lot of privilege within it that you didn't see in other segments of society. It made me realize the extent to which language isolates people in their own different slices of reality. After all, when your language skills are limited, you end up just going to the places where people are good at speaking English.

One day in the fall of 2013, walking by the Chiang Kai-shek Memorial, I noticed several dozen people gathered by the south gate. Wooden crates had been set up as a makeshift stage among the shadows cast by a monument to a dead dictator.

The performer was a man with long hair, torn jeans, and glasses. He played a guitar, which he looped and added effects to with an array of electronics around him — a combination of rock and glitch. He manipulated his gear with a great deal of showmanship, using a cell phone strapped to his arm that he would tap on and a large glowing ring on his finger that he waved around to control some of his gear.

But it was the second act that really drew me in. A man with close-cropped hair and thin features put a box on his head, and over the sound of klaxons playing from a stereo, he began a monologue about some future, post-nuclear apocalypse. The tone was humorous, even self-deprecating in some way. Yet the implication was that Taiwan could, in fact, see something like this as a possible future. That was the reason why people protested, wasn't it? To try to hold off the futures that they didn't want for themselves, for those around them; to try to create those they did.

It held me hypnotized — I had gotten into noise and performance art while in New York City, but I had never seen anything like this before. It seemed in and of itself to be some kind of protest.

"What's going on here?" I asked a girl who was going around getting names from attendees. She responded to me in Mandarin. A short girl wearing a knit cap and woolen sweater, she had a distinctive birthmark below one of her eyes. I could tell she was a bit younger than I was.

"Sorry, I don't totally understand," I said to her. "My Mandarin is really bad." I had to ask her to slow down. She switched to English.

"Where are you from?" she asked. As it turned out, she had fluent English with a slight British accent. Oftentimes, accents in Taiwan vary based on what country your first English teacher is from.

"New York," I said. She seemed surprised at that.

"How old are you?"

"Twenty-one."

"I'm nineteen," she said. She laughed. "What's your name?"

I told her my Chinese name. "My friends call me Ah-Qiu."
"I'm Yuli."

Yuli introduced me to a few of her other friends that night. What I had stumbled across was a weekly anti-nuclear demonstration. And there it was, somehow. That's how it began, and the course of my life changed from then. Fate; being in the right place at the right time; being in the wrong place at the wrong time; call it what you will. Three months later, Yuli would be one of the people that stormed the Legislative Yuan — Taiwan's parliament — as one of the first wave of occupiers during the Sunflower Movement. She and I would be among the first three members of *Daybreak*.

I started attending the weekly protest, and joined the reading group that Yuli was part of. She was a medical student at a university located on Yangming Mountain overlooking Taipei, and I found myself trekking up the mountain several times a week, despite how far it was from both where I lived and where I was studying. They read quite a wide-ranging set of texts — everything from books on the nature of consciousness to radical political philosophy. I was a bit surprised, actually, to find myself reading Marx in Taiwan. I had imagined that the legacy of the KMT's anti-Communism would be more pervasive among young people, but that wasn't the case at all.

A lot of the texts were things I had read before, texts that they themselves read through English translation. That was a privilege, I guess, of being from New York. I knew myself that one of the reasons they found me interesting was because of that background.

My Mandarin got better. It was fragmentary in the beginning, but I didn't need to think before I said anything: one of the benefits of being a former native speaker, Mandarin actually predated English as my mother tongue. Starting to talk with Yuli and the others in Mandarin instead of English opened up new possibilities for me, too, and it felt as though I was rediscovering a part of myself, a part long-forgotten or which I had never really known. But what I enjoyed most of all was just getting to know Taiwanese people my own age. Young people the world over had the same concerns, for the most part — we all knew that we lacked the future that our parents were promised from early on, and so all we had were our bonds with each other.

Looking back, I realize that Taiwan was in some way primed for a social uprising, though I failed to realize it at the time. Young people were all talking about ideas in reading groups like the one I had taken to frequenting on campuses all across the island, and were bonding with each other over the conditions that we all faced. The groups themselves were becoming increasingly interlinked and connected in a way that would allow for collective mobilization.

That things were headed toward an explosion — what would later be remembered as a generational moment — should have been obvious. I had long been convinced of the potential in the intersection of art and politics, and art, film, and music were all going new and exciting places.

It was a time when something of an activist subculture was developing, too, in urban centers, and it seemed like every hipster coffee shop was plastered with banners, with some even hosting talks on political issues; others had backrooms that could serve as spaces for planning political interventions — we often went to one such place by National Taiwan University, which was run by a PhD student in Taiwanese literature and funded by professors there.

There were exhibitions that we all went to as well, and movies and documentaries that were hotly discussed because of their focus on social issues. Some people were so passionate about film festivals that they might attend all of the films that were being shown, skipping class to do so. Some attendees would leave tickets they had reserved or bought for friends who had canceled so that others could watch the films and educate themselves on whatever social issue was being documented. In music there was a sudden transition, seemingly overnight, from broody melancholic post-rock to angry, often masculine indie rock with lyrics that expressed frustration at not having the opportunities that previous generations had, at having the future stolen away and their dreams crushed; at shows by activist bands where everyone congregated to discuss politics, the band members themselves often discussed similar issues in between songs. If English speakers existed in a parallel reality, then the activists also comprised a world within a world. Certainly, activist subcultures existed the world over, but I had never seen anything on the scale of what I saw in Taipei. It was only a matter of time before it spilled out into the public at large.

It all came to be remembered as a hopeful thing, and yet what's often forgotten was how apocalyptic it all seemed at the time. Why else would that many people have taken to the streets if not for the sense of doom that hung over their heads? Nothing is poetry until it's over, until it is safely dead and past. In the moment, it's just messy incommensurable reality, exceeding any capacity to capture it in language. Then, later, accessing it in memory, it all becomes aestheticized, sanitized. We remember a particular version of the past — even of who we were — rather than what truly was.

Young people were genuinely convinced that we would not have a future unless we took action. This led to a sense of desperation, and when you're desperate, you're willing to take risks — even to put your life on the line.

"318" — as March 18 later came to be known — began with a demonstration at the Legislative Yuan against a trade bill that was signed with China, and eventually turned into a spontaneous occupation of the legislature. Public anger arose from the fact that the bill, controversial in itself, was pushed through the legislature within thirty seconds by the KMT, circumventing oversight processes — something taken as a sign of the KMT's resurgent authoritarianism. The KMT was in power again, after all, and they still hadn't let go of the past.

I wasn't at the demonstration that day, because I was eating dinner with a friend. I saw the pictures of the charge into the Legislative Yuan on social media. I was a bit dismissive at first: "I'm sure they'll be driven out in a few hours," I remember commenting to my dinner partner when the news broke. I had become cynical from having spent the last few years drifting around protests. Still, after we had finished, I got antsy. I was never one to pass up a chance for action. Then I heard from our circle of friends that Yuli was in the Legislative Yuan. I would have to go. So that was it. I decided to take that gamble. I jumped into a taxi and told the driver to head straight there. It was shortly after midnight.

There were many stories told later on about drivers that took students to the Legislative Yuan for free, or who had kind words of support for them. Mine wasn't like that. "Bunch of kids, just making trouble," he muttered when I told him where I was going. He took me anyway.

I got out of the taxi by Jinan South Road, the part of town where most government buildings were located, such as the executive branch, legislature, and various ministries, in the vicinity of Shandao Temple in a series of drab buildings that were largely built for functional purposes or which had had other historical uses. The legislature had housed a girl's high school during the Japanese colonial period, for instance, while the office building across from it had been a prison for political detainees during the White Terror.

By that point, several hundred had gathered. Somebody was giving speeches on a stage that had been set up during the earlier protest. Not too long after, someone else started playing songs on a guitar. Eighty percent of the people there looked like students.

I found people I knew; Zhexiong and Jian, two of the students from the reading group, who I only knew distantly. They didn't seem too surprised to see me. For some time, I had been this strange person you ran into on the fringes of protests. In the absence of anything else to do, we sat down on the side of the road. I checked my phone and noticed that one of my friends from the Japanese anti-nuclear movement had shared a Facebook status about the occupation. I saw that the status had been written by Zhexiong.

I sent her a message: "Funny thing, I'm sitting in front of the occupation with Zhexiong right now. How do you know him?" As it turned out, she didn't actually know him personally. The post had gone viral, had close to 9,500 likes and 15,000 shares, and had been translated into over thirty languages — and here I was just sitting across from Zhexiong, who had written it and organized crowdsourced translations of it from the original Chinese.

"What have I stumbled onto?" I recall asking myself that at the time. I later learned that Taiwan had the highest Facebook penetration of anywhere in the world. Sixty percent of the population was on the platform, as a result of which social media was the center of a lot of organizing, and I realized for the first time that the activism I was encountering in Taiwan was unlike anything else I'd ever seen.

The occupiers had taken over the legislative chambers and barricaded the exits. They were surrounded by riot police, who were poised throughout the rest of the building and kept trying to break down the barriers the students had built out of chairs and other objects they'd found.

In the meantime, others like me had heard what was happening and rushed over to the Legislative Yuan. Even if the building itself was full of riot police, we in turn had the police surrounded on the outside of the building. It was a stand-off, taking the form of a series of layered, nested confrontations.

The neon lights of storefronts and streetlamps were the only source of illumination in the night, throwing everything into a sepia shading. It wasn't a sight unfamiliar to me. It's always when night falls that you see action in a protest.

The crowd began to push against the gates, trying to force its way past the riot police and into the parking lot, then onward to drive the police out of the building. As the crowd grew more and more brazen, I hung around at the back. I guess I still feared arrest, in those days.

When demonstrators started climbing over the fencing around the perimeter and forcing open the front gate, I found myself surveying the scene from the top of a wall that I had climbed onto. Nearby, Zhexiong stood on top of a news van with a megaphone, issuing directions to those who were trying to force down the front gate. His silhouette is still imprinted on my memory. Whether it was Yuli on the inside or Zhexiong on the outside, I was struck by what an impressive cast of people I had stumbled upon, all younger than me. Near the end of the night, I was trying to sleep, laying my head against the hood of a car parked in the Legislative Yuan parking lot, long after the gates had been broken open by the crowd. I drifted in and out of consciousness.

Then, unable to sleep, I looked up. I noticed people holding sunflowers up against the darkness. It was nearly dawn and I was exhausted, but I was there the moment the Sunflower Movement was born.

A few days passed and I struggled to make sense of the circumstances. Just drifting around protests wasn't enough. I knew too little about Taiwanese politics. So I read. I took out books from the university library — Chinese or English, it didn't matter by then — and brought them with me to the Legislative Yuan. By that point, a small occupation had sprouted up around the complex. I would sit there, talk to whoever was around, and read.

There's a sort of freedom in occupied space that one seldom finds elsewhere in capitalist society, a utopianism almost, as suddenly everyone is energized by a spirit of mutual aid and collective care. Donations of all sorts of supplies came in, everything from lunchboxes to bottles of water, medical supplies, and even condoms. Services offered included everything from free rides from those who had come up from Central and Southern Taiwan to mental health services, or even just help with homework. This was a way out of the unfreedom of commodified reality, in which everything carried a price tag, and in which all human relations were only the vehicle for some kind of exchange it seemed to me. Perhaps occupied space is the only place where genuine, human relations can flourish.

I realized that the government buildings around the legislature were in some ways a no-space. There was no reason for these buildings, or the amount of urban space they occupied, to exist except to maintain the stable operations of the state out of the reach of everyday citizens. And yet here was all this space — which normally only existed as a bland, sterile no-man's land — being put to use in the visceral manner of lived politics — closer to the "original" state of politics, I wanted to believe, which is to say, politics in a state of innocence. There was a euphoria to that time spent wandering around occupied space, then. This is the truest form of human relation, I told myself: the only place where I myself could feel some meaningful sense of connection to my fellow human being. It reminded me of my own attempt to recover my first nature — long since covered over by my second nature — by coming to Taiwan. To reclaim the world: that was what I wanted, no?

In the meantime, the inside of the legislature had become the nerve center of the movement. That was where the leadership core was, which called the shots for the movement as a whole. It became a strange panopticon-like space, where cameras were rolling continuously 24/7. It was necessary to get the news out about what was going on, and the movement transformed into a media spectacle. Despite this, the gap between the inside and outside was growing increasingly large. Some protesters grew more and more dissatisfied with the decisions made by those inside of the legislature, particularly as the media began to hone in on a few key figures that they dubbed the leaders of the movement, while for those on the inside, it was difficult to truly know what was going on outside — though messages could be passed using cell phones, via the Internet, or along with the supplies necessary to keep the occupation going, an information gap still arose. In some way, I could see that the dynamic of the movement was driven forward by this push and pull between the inside and outside, the core and the periphery. Strange how this often seems to be the driving motor of world history, as with the inward and outward rotation of an oceanic storm.

After about a week, it looked as though coverage of the movement was starting to dry up as the media shifted back to its usual diet of dashcam footage and celebrity gossip. The government, in the meantime, kept silent, knowing that if it simply waited long enough, the energy of the movement would burn out. There started to be talk of a need for further action — for something that would escalate the situation and force an answer from the government. The demand was that the trade bill be repealed.

It began in a very mundane way. The leader of the reading group, Tianyang, wanted us to go to an event on protest tactics at Cafe Philo, an activist cafe. But Yuli, who had gone into the legislature for a few days and since come back out, had cut in at that point. "We're not going there," she said in our shared chatroom. "The National Taiwan University, Xuzhou campus, that's where we are going." She was adamant, but refused to explain what it was all about, and shut down any attempt by Tianyang to protest, only saying it was absolutely necessary and that we shouldn't go to the talk — that this was our "duty." Eventually, she talked the rest of the group into it. She could be very persuasive when she needed to be.

That's how I got caught up in the chaos around Executive Yuan — events later termed "324" because they took place in the early morning hours of 24 March — and unexpectedly found myself charging down the executive branch of a government. I didn't have any real sense of what the risk level would be or the scale of the response, but it would later be remembered as the largest use of police force in Taiwan since the end of martial law.

I was taken aback when we got to the Department of Social Sciences. It had been turned into an off-site staging ground for actions. There were dozens of students there, maybe around fifty, all running around. We were split into five-man cells and told to exchange phone numbers, then we all wrote down our phone numbers so that we could be registered into a mass texting system. It was already rather chaotic.

Anyone with a student ID — even someone like me with only an international student ID — was allowed in. It was hard to imagine undercover police didn't know about it, but everything had been kept under wraps. Yuli herself had not known the exact plan until a few hours beforehand; someone she knew and trusted had told her to, in turn, gather people that she knew and could rely on to maintain complete secrecy. The majority of those present had been pulled there through friend groups and networks and did not know what the plan was, though this wasn't that unusual, as a lot was done through person-to-person contact and communication was kept deliberately cryptic. After all, we knew organizers' phones were likely being tapped. The secrecy was a matter of controversy later on, and some claimed they had been more or less tricked into the action. But, for the record, I didn't think it was unjustified. Sometimes you've got to do what you've got to do.

There were to be three teams of approximately fifty people tasked with charging the front, side, and back doors of the Executive Yuan. The group I was in was the back door team. We were told to split up and meet at a designated location in order to start the charge at 7:25pm.

Night was rapidly falling. The city was quickly covered in neon light after the sun set. It was strange walking through the sprawling occupation that had sprouted up around the legislature and other nearby government buildings, running into other people who had also been at the Department of Social Sciences and trying to act as if everything was normal. "See you later," we usually said if it was someone we knew. If it wasn't, we just nodded to each other silently.

Whatever happened later that night, I knew there was the risk of death. just as I knew that in a revolution there are times when you have to decide if it's worth sacrificing your life — sometimes just within the span of a few seconds.

We went for something to eat and, if memory serves, got convenience-store food. I recall only buying some bread because I anticipated having to run and I didn't want to feel sick. I wasn't sure why, but everyone else seemed to find that funny.

"What are you doing?" asked Yuli.

"Can't fight on an empty — or too full — stomach, no?" I laughed. But there was no denying that I was nervous — that we were nervous. It was hard to keep it out of my voice.

We converged on a street corner maybe two or three hundred feet from the back door of the Executive Yuan. We were the first group to arrive. Yuli made us all huddle along the corner of a wall so we were less visible to the police, but as we did so, I noticed a large bus full of riot police drive by. I started talking to Emma, someone in the group I only knew distantly. She and some others were talking about whether the police had found out about our plans.

"What do you think are the actual chances for us succeeding here?" I asked. "You saw that, right?" I asked, meaning the bus.

"Probably we don't stand a chance," said Yuli. "Maybe we'll all be arrested in a short while." I was impressed by how nonchalant she was about it.

"I don't think there's any way the police didn't know about this," I said.

"Through monitoring social media?"

"Or undercover police," I said.

Why had I not backed out? I had been caught up in the moment. I wouldn't have wanted to back out even if there'd been some way of doing so. This was what it meant to live genuinely in the moment, to be truly alive, wasn't it? I looked around and saw Tianyang pacing. Someone had asked him how we would know when to charge. "Someone will come here and tell us when," he said.

I don't know how much time passed after that. During these kinds of things, the flow of time seems to dilate. I never saw who it was that ordered us to charge. Later on, I had to check that there was in fact someone who came with that order, but suddenly we were running, a few dozen students. The police were the least of my worries now. I was surprised by how light I felt, running in the streets, sprinting with all my might.

And then we were pressing up against the police and their riot shields, trying to push them back. The rest is a flash in my memory.

「警察！後退！警察！後退！」

I was stuck somewhere in the middle of the group. The left flank was collapsing, it looked like the people on that side were going to be crushed by the police. I began screaming out, "To the left! We need more people on the left!"

I don't think anyone heard me. The automatic gate began shutting, but I was too far in the back to see it with my own eyes. I just heard the noise of it closing suddenly. I was propelled back into someone from the reading group I didn't know, and we tried to force back the police side-by-side, pushing up against the backs of the people in front of us as others pushed us from behind. I learned later that several people had gotten injured when the automatic gate closed on them; in the heat of the moment I didn't see any of this. It was just all so many bodies converging on each other, colliding in space.

Without warning, the police were suddenly on us from behind, with their black batons and body armor.

Reconstructing what happened later on, this could only have been five minutes after the charge had begun, but time itself seemed not to be a factor at that point. There they were all of a sudden, all these black carapaces beating down on us with their batons and shields. We were all wearing black, the color of the protests. Many of us were wearing black shirts that read: "Fuck the Government." It was black against black.

I ended up being ejected from the center of the charge. I assumed a look of not really understanding what I was doing. A policeman shoved me aside, and I ended up in the surrounding crowd of bystanders. I remember hearing Tianyang shouting at the police, "In the annals of history, it's you who will go down as the criminals!" as he was dragged away. It was the kind of long-winded thing he would say.

Our charge had attracted attention from a crowd given the number of people around the occupation encampment every night. As some of the bystanders were also students, I blended in, Yuli was also forced out of the charge, and I pulled her toward me.

I remember being frozen in shock for several moments as Yuli and I stood there, isolated, while a throng of police surrounded our group of friends. We were cut off and had no way of knowing what had happened to them. Had they been beaten by the police? Were they hurt? These were the kinds of thoughts that ran through my head.

"Lie down! Lie down! Lie down!" Yuli shouted at me, bringing my thoughts back to the immediate moment. A number of students who had been forced out of the charge were lying down on the ground in front of the riot police, who had surrounded the rest of the group. Clever thinking, whoever had come up with the idea: the riot police would have to step on us if they wanted to get out. I lay down next to

Yuli, linking arms with her on my left and with a girl I didn't know on my right.

In the tension of the moment, Yuli began crying, leaving me unsure of what to say. "It'll be alright, it'll be alright," I kept repeating, rather unconvincingly.

From then on, it was a waiting game. While we lay down on the ground, the riot police had arranged themselves so that they were facing the crowd with their shields directed outward. Another flank of police faced inward in a circle, with their shields directed at those they had waded through. Police stood back to back with each other, holding shields in either direction. But they couldn't leave and drag away our friends because they would have to trample us to get out. And because we had been quick to block their path of escape, the crowd behind us were able to prevent the riot police from leaving altogether, even if they had decided to trample us.

The resulting stand-off at the back of the Executive Yuan would last for close to three hours, but it felt like a brief moment. I spent a lot of it staring at the night sky, in which no stars were visible, and trying to make small talk.

Eventually, people began to trade off places and take shifts lying on the ground. At one point, an elderly woman who seemed to have a heart condition arrived and insisted on trading places with the girl on my right, despite my continually urging her not to do so because of her health. We got her to leave after a while.

Members of the Referendum Alliance, a Taiwanese independence group that had run a small occupation next to the Legislative Yuan for the past few years, also turned up during this time, bringing ladders in order to scale the gate and try to make their way into the building through the windows. A few managed to get in, and for a while there was some scuffling between alliance members (who tended to be elderly), some students who were trying to protect them, and the police. In the end, the police seized the ladders.

The police finally broke their cordon around 10pm, letting our friends go. The crowd wasn't willing to relent, so I guess they had decided to abandon attempts to arrest those who had been surrounded. We were let off the hook — none of us were arrested. We had been lucky.

I had to corroborate the story of exactly what had happened with Zhexiong later. He had been directing people in front of the Executive Yuan rather than with us as we were storming the back gate. The charge by the front door team had succeeded in breaking through the barricades, and some of the protesters managed to climb over the barriers by placing towels on top of them, eventually forcing one of them apart. If anything, they were perhaps too successful in forcing an opening, and it became a problem that there were too many people trying to surge in, as many of the protesters who had just been hanging out in the area started entering the Executive Yuan's parking lot.

When we got to the front gate of the building, it was just past 10:30pm. Police were blocking the entrance to the building itself, but in the parking lot there was a mix of protesters and police, who were trying to force people out — though they hadn't gotten to the point of using overwhelming force yet. It was only later that the police violence the night is remembered for began.

It looked more like a war zone than an attempted occupation. To make it in and out as a group, we linked arms and weaved through the wreckage of police barriers strewn everywhere. I remember seeing some cloth banners that had been thrown up, but I don't remember what any of them said. Everything was sheathed in a dim red light. Seeing as there wasn't anything we could do, we went back to the Department of Social Sciences. The water cannons began firing at half past midnight. At that time, we were trying to rest up, in case something else happened. It was me who first noticed the pictures on Facebook when the image of the man, his face bloodied from being beaten by police batons, began circulating.

We waited around for some time to keep track of ongoing developments, and had a tense discussion about whether we should go back to the Executive Yuan building and whether doing so would have any effect on the course of events or if we would simply end up getting ourselves hurt. As there didn't seem to be much we could do, we broke up and vowed to keep in contact and to plan future actions. I took a taxi home.

I'll probably never forget what Tianyang said that night. "Well, it looks like the monster that hasn't shown its face in twenty years has returned." The authoritarian past was back, maybe it had never gone away.

I went back in the afternoon the next day. Strangely, one of the first people I encountered was an old man with a shock of white hair who I had seen in the background of a photo in the news showing that he had been beaten bloody by the police. The old man was, for some reason, still standing in the exact same place he had been when the photo was taken. But I was struck — appalled — by how otherwise empty it was around the occupation site. I had expected people to be out in force. As it was, it wouldn't have been hard for the police to clear the occupation, had they wanted to.

One of the cops that night had injured several dozens of students, just by himself, but he was never identified. I still remember catching a glimpse of him before the violence broke out, he seemed *eager* to crack skulls open, and I remember, too, how impatient he seemed to be, tapping his baton with a grimace. There were some that hungered for violence against the students, I realized, and what perhaps shocked me even more was the public response. This was the largest concerted use of police force since the martial law period, yet public reaction showed that many sided with the authorities. Online commentators praised the actions of police, blow by blow, as they lashed out against protesters with batons, fired tear gas, or blasted them with water cannons. The protesters deserved it! That there were some who found such joy in violence horrified me especially as it was against students, who were traditionally seen as having a "pure" role in Taiwanese society.

Even among activists themselves, the events of that night were controversial. When I was talking to demonstrators around the Legislative Yuan two or three days later, asking them how they felt about the attempted Executive Yuan occupation, many expressed their disapproval; they felt the police were justified in their actions. Why? "Because it wasn't our space," said one person I asked, shaking his head. "We didn't belong there."

I felt like throwing up my arms in frustration. The Executive Yuan occupation was deemed illegitimate because it had been premeditated, whereas the Legislative Yuan occupation was seen as legitimate because it was perceived as spontaneous. It may, in fact, have been lucky that the Legislative Yuan occupation and the Executive Yuan occupation became disentangled in the media, as the fallout from the Executive Yuan occupation did not end up discrediting the movement as a whole.

Still, the failed Executive Yuan occupation made Taiwan the focus of international coverage in a way that the Legislative Yuan didn't. It's blood that draws the attention of the media. Osamu Dazai compared journalists with terrorists once, and I think he was right. Funny that I was on the path to becoming a journalist myself. But I still believed that what we were trying to do that night was heroic. Sometimes people have to be willing to go against the tide for any change to happen in society. Perhaps what is needed most is for some to be prepared to become enemies of the people, for the sake of the people.

It made me realize that I had become cynical over the past few years. It didn't feel as if anything I had done in life, any social movement I had participated in, any action I had undertaken to try to break the impasse of society at large, had had any real effect. It was hard for me not to feel moved by all this.

I would go to the occupation encampment daily after classes let out and read until it was dark. Sometimes I would stay at night and continue to read in the dim lighting from the neon storefronts. During this time, we only heard sporadically from Yuli, who had gone back into the legislature. At that point, she had taken to staying on the inside full-time. They didn't have reliable access to the Internet within the Legislative Yuan. There were rumors that the government was disrupting it. Once in a while, I would see a Facebook status from her, but she didn't respond to any of my messages. It was fairly easy to get inside. The occupiers let in a certain number of people each day. So some people in our group saw her, but I didn't hear very much about her from anyone.

Attempts were made by the media to paint the students as troublemakers who had seized control of the legislature for no really substantive reason, merely the desire to be the center of attention. Sometimes the reporting on female protesters was overtly sexualized, suggesting that they simply wished to be in the spotlight and to look good in front of the cameras in order to attract boyfriends. Meanwhile, the male protest leaders were framed in terms of masculine bravado, a different kind of sexualization. Well, the Taiwanese media was nothing if not misogynistic, and Taiwanese politics nothing if not male-dominated.

Sometimes young people are willing to stake their blood for the sake of society as a whole, but that doesn't mean everyone will come to appreciate it. And maybe that's just the way history has been — that's why protest movements always seem to be full of young people. Tensions ran high sometimes. Someone slit their wrists in front of the Legislative Yuan and wrote a big character poster with their blood. Someone else tried to self-immolate. A month earlier, someone had tried to crash a truck into the Presidential Office in an act of protest, but no one died. That came later.

March 30 — "330" — twelve days after the start of the occupation, would later come to be remembered as the movement's high point. Five hundred thousand, some 2 percent of the Taiwanese population, would gather on the streets of Taipei that day. The demonstration had been called for a few days in advance by the group inside of the Legislative Yuan, with the money to organize the event apparently materializing from spontaneous donations. It was all quite amazing, yet at the time it felt like a bit of an anticlimax.

I met up with Tianyang, Zhexiong, Emma, and all the others, and we went and sat down on the road in front of Taipei Main Station as though it were a picnic or some other outing. Yuli didn't join us. We hadn't seen or heard from her for weeks by then. She stopped responding to messages. At one point, I remember seeing her post on Facebook, apropos of nothing, "Are you willing to DIE for your country?" I had asked Emma, who was closer to her, what she had thought. "I think Yuli… is broken." She meant mentally. Yuli's parents had even come to Taipei at some point to look for her. But she just ignored them.

We played cards. And then at 6pm, suddenly everyone just packed up and left. Strange how often it seemed to be that way in Asia. It was a bit frightening how quickly half a million people could disperse. Looking back, I realize that it could have been a revolutionary situation. What if half a million people had just refused to leave? The police would have tried to use force to drive them out. Then things could have rapidly escalated. The Legislative Yuan occupiers, however, were maybe a bit too intent on keeping the movement respectable. They asked the crowd to disperse in an orderly fashion once it was 6pm, and they did just that.

Two days later, the Grey Wolf turned up.

The Grey Wolf had been a gangster who had conducted political assassinations for the KMT in the 1980s. He was the "Godfather" of the Black Forest Gang, or so they claimed.

The Black Forest Gang was one of Taiwan's major gangs, involved in everything from drug trafficking to racketeering and the like, but it had originally consisted of waishengren that met together on basketball courts in Taipei and banded together to protect themselves. They were kids then, of course, who had been thrown into a new environment after the Chinese Civil War led them to come to Taiwan with their parents. But what begins as a means of self-protection can quickly become another system of oppression.

The Grey Wolf had been involved in the killing of Taiwanese American journalist Henry Chen in California in 1984, after which the FBI had become involved, and he was arrested, dealing a blow to the credibility of the KMT.

After that, Grey Wolf had fled to China, only returning to Taiwan after many years in exile. He had since reinvented himself as a pro-China politician. In spite of being a fringe politician and a former political assassin, he was quite close to the sister of the president, who was also the chair of the KMT.

He showed up with several hundred of his acolytes in tow after announcing that he would drive out the students by force, calling them traitors to the great Han race, among other things. He and his lackeys set up a stage on Zhongxiao West Road and tried to provoke the nearby protesters into an altercation. Those who strayed too close to the Grey Wolf and his colleagues were attacked and beaten. Though a large number of police had amassed nearby, they did nothing to stop the assaults, despite the fact they were taking place outside the National Police Agency. There was nothing surprising in this; the Grey Wolf had friends in high places — the president, the one pushing for the trade bill to begin with, being among them.

The next ten days after that were quiet. Since no occupation could last forever, the students announced that they would be withdrawing on April 10. When they left, the crowd outside cheered them on, celebrating them as heroes. It was over, I thought. Time to go home. That wasn't actually the end though, as it turned out. There was an afterlife to the movement that lasted for most of the remainder of April, now generally forgotten. It may have been after the withdrawal from the Legislative Yuan that tensions between protesters and police ran highest, since there was no sense of a clear direction to the movement anymore.

When some refused to withdraw from the legislature on the night of April 10, police force was used to remove them. During the tumult that followed, Dr Tsay, the leader of the Referendum Alliance, ran into traffic and was struck by a scooter. As a result, close to a thousand people gathered outside of the Zhongzheng First Police Precinct that night, surrounding the station and refusing to allow the police to leave. It was only after the chief of the precinct came out and announced that he would be resigning that the crowds dispersed.

I remember arriving that night, alone, and finding that the police station had been covered in posters with slogans against police brutality written on them. The gathering had begun as a spontaneous development through calls to take action on the online forum PTT. That so many people had come together within just a few short hours was a sign of the intensity of public outrage. Just as people can turn on a movement, at other times rage can crystallize powerfully against the powers that be. It was all two sides of the same coin — mercurial as the abstraction that is "the people" often is.

But the demonstration became another controversial issue in the media. Some rallied behind the police in the name of law and order, depicting them as the defenders of public morality and the protesters as antisocial elements. The suggestion was that protesters were disrupting normative social harmony, and the media harped on the fact that the police were being forced to work overtime because of the protests when they had families and lives of their own. I was used to a political context in which protesters would have likely just set the police station on fire — and while that had happened previously in Taiwanese history, clearly it wasn't something on the cards in present-day, democratic Taiwan.

This was typical for Taiwanese society — for any society, really. You can push, but there's such a thing as "fear of freedom." Accomplishing anything meaningful politically always entails a struggle against the everyday and the common morality of society. It takes a lot of energy and determination to swim against the current. I remember hearing many stories of conflicts between families then, children having to fight it out with their parents. That's the only way society changes, I suspect.

It reminded me of Lu Xun's "Diary of a Madman." The history of humanity, which is to say, all of written history, was all just tens of thousands of years of cannibalism, wasn't it? Of parents eating their children. Or children eating each other. I am sure Aoi would have agreed. Sometimes a society eats its young alive, I've come to realize. Someone has to be on the chopping block of history — and sometimes it's us.

"It is you," *the emptiness* said to me. It is us, isn't it, V?

The resignation wasn't the end of it. The former chair of the Democratic Progressive Party (DPP), Lin Yi-hsiung, whose own children had been killed by the KMT during the martial law period, began a hunger strike against nuclear energy. Much later, I would be told by people who knew him that this was an attempt to prevent a loss of momentum after the withdrawal from the Legislative Yuan, and to ensure that there would be tangible results from the movement.

A clash broke out between police and demonstrators outside of the Legislative Yuan on the day that Lin began his hunger strike. Daily protests took place in Daan Park, and another mass rally was called for April 27. The plan was to occupy Zhongxiao West Road and refuse to leave. Fifty thousand gathered, the majority of whom did in fact just leave when it got late. It wasn't so different from March 30. It felt a bit like a picnic, and many people brought their families. But at night, the police came in with water cannons for those who hadn't left. I'm told that doctors in Taiwan never expected to see the use of high-pressure water cannons, powerful enough to affect internal organs, after the end of martial law. It happened more than once in those weeks, both then in April and during 324.

Lin stopped his hunger strike a few days later. He didn't die. I still wonder whether, if he had, there would have been armed revolution in the streets. There were some moments when it appeared as though he was ready to. People were talking about violence being on the table if he did. But, in the end, again the movement died.

I met Neil around then. Neil was the friend of a friend from high school. Upstate New York was only so large, it sometimes seemed.

He was a graduate of a liberal arts school, and we had met at a party some years ago — an event for a magazine — though neither of us had any real recollection of the encounter. He had seen that I was posting about the Legislative Yuan occupation on Facebook and, because he freelanced as a journalist, messaged me in the hopes that I could get him more information.

Like me, being from New York had opened a lot of doors for him in Taiwan, such is the cultural cachet of the city. The first day we met was two days after 324. "It's been fascinating," I remember him saying of the occupation. "You don't usually see something like this in New York."

I agreed with him. I certainly hadn't either.

He towered over those around him. He was tall and muscular, always wearing ill-fitting button-down shirts. It made him stand out almost everywhere he went in Taiwan. Even around the occupation, he had a way of attracting glances. Being white in Asia does that for you, I guess. We spent an afternoon walking around the occupation site and talking before he took the train back to Tainan. I didn't admit to him then that I had been part of the charge on 318 and 324; I still didn't trust him fully.

Talking with him that day, I recall thinking that this was probably the longest conversation I'd had with anyone in English for quite a while. I even had the sense that my English was starting to degrade. Back then, I was happy just to see another American. We had a lot of shared intellectual interests, regarding Asian politics among other things. We kept in touch after. It occurred to both of us that there was a need for better news coverage in Taiwan, and one day he just suggested it to me.

"We could do so much better," he said. "Come on, don't you just feel like taking the world by storm?"

He had a point. Much of the media establishment that reported on Taiwan was old and lackluster. Not much of anything had been written about the social movement in English — international news coverage that month was almost exclusively focused on a Malaysian flight that had simply disappeared over the Indian Ocean. Besides, most of the people who reported on Taiwan weren't really interested in Taiwan itself but, reflecting Taiwan's global obscurity, as part and parcel of their reporting on the bigger issue: China. Many of the perspectives about the movement were written from Beijing's perspective. I had some misgivings no doubt, but let myself be talked into it. *Daybreak* was never my idea, or my project, at least in the beginning.

The original idea was just to start a joint blog, but I felt that wasn't really interesting or wide-ranging enough. Since I knew so many activists, why not pull in some of them, too? Yuli had been out of the legislature for some time by that point, I suggested to her that this was a project she could be involved in. Besides, it struck me that the project needed the involvement of at least one person who had stayed in the legislature for the duration of the movement, otherwise it lacked legitimacy — it would just be another expat blog.

Neil had been living in Tainan for the past year, taking language classes at National Cheng Kung University. He had gone to the south because it was cheaper, and so, since Neil had come up to Taipei so many times during the movement and we were hoping to get out of there for a change of scene, we met up in Tainan, where we wrote a pretentious manifesto in a bar proclaiming the importance of *Daybreak*'s foundation in the grandest of terms. Yuli didn't seem interested in the writing process at all, chatting with Neil's then girlfriend while the two of us hunched over a laptop. The next day we all had hangovers.

The founding members included Zhexiong, who had become something of an Internet celebrity by that point due to the crowdfunded status update; Yufang, an anarchist I knew who was trying to start a commune in Taoyuan; and Cheng, a Taiwanese PhD candidate in New York who had been organizing solidarity rallies, and I met through a Japanese friend from my time in Tokyo. I later found out Cheng was living a double life as a famous lesbian poet in Taiwan, though I knew her as a graduate student initially. Nigel, the oldest of us, in his thirties, was the friend of a friend. Some of us had just gotten to know each other through the Internet in the weeks around the movement. Social media could still be a way of connecting people and groups in those years of occupation-style movements; this became much harder after Facebook began monetizing content, making it so that you had to pay if you wanted to reach anyone.

The first meeting we had, strangely enough, took place in the Taipei Veteran's Memorial Hospital in the dead of night.

Yufang was working there at the time. He suggested that his office in the hospital would be a good place to have the meeting, as it had more than one computer that we would use in order to Skype with people overseas. That was the first time we all came together. Another time, I took them to Brother Tseng's bar, and we all sang karaoke. Brother Tseng later commented to me that my friends all seemed to be hipsters.

It was fun, I guess, in the beginning. It was the first time I'd been part of a group in this way. That is, I had always been searching for groups to be a part of, but I never felt that I fit anywhere. It was something new, creating a group of one's own.

Neil claimed he liked Taiwan. It was "small, but charming," he said. Not that he would ever consider living there long-term. I came to find his way of looking at the world very simple. It was very *American*. But he was smart and knew how to go places. It was fun for a while, and in the beginning we got along alright. I couldn't deny that there was a part of me that felt isolated living in Taiwan as an American. Not that I had ever felt very American. But there were certain things that I couldn't talk about with others — like American politics, for one. No one understood where I came from. Looking back, I actually came to trust Neil quite quickly.

Most of the time, he lived in Tainan, while I was in Taipei. But we chatted daily on Facebook, sending each other articles, or discussing what we were reading. Even just our emotional lives. I wasn't dating anyone at the time or trying to, but Neil was dating around. The usual ups and downs of two men in our early twenties. Maybe now that I was in Taiwan, I was just looking for some kind of analogue to David. Perhaps I was just desperate for someone to confide in, seeing as Taiwan was an unfamiliar place.

Neil was a good deal more outgoing than I. If he walked into a room, he would make it a point to talk with everyone. As for me, I had always been a bit more withdrawn. A lot of my friends were, in fact, much more outgoing. Sometimes,

Neil's behavior was a bit obnoxious in fact. But I liked that about him, at least then.

We were an odd pair and didn't have a lot in common, apart from shared intellectual interests regarding Asia. He probably thought of me as a hipster, and I thought of him as one of those more polished types that usually end up in DC think tanks. He wasn't exactly interested in the leftism that ended up becoming part of the publication, but leftism was a sexy word in those days, in the aftermath of Occupy Wall Street. Somehow Occupy had become what it had claimed to oppose — a logo, an ad, a sign. Protest is perhaps all too easy to commodify, to aestheticize.

We did share being from the same part of New York, as he was from another place not too far from where I had grown up, in the vast span of suburban nothingness. I thought of that as maybe the basis of our mutual bond. Possibly he could sense my being from an unremarkable place. Ironically, he seemed to envy me for living in the capital while he was in Tainan, just as he was always a bit anxious about the fact that he wasn't from New York City itself, just one of the nameless towns around it. Well, every place has its own endless layers of centers and peripheries, and sometimes I had felt that way as well, so I understood his anxiety. He sometimes seemed to be a bit envious of my knowledge of art and culture, too; that was something he didn't have. That lack of knowledge became very evident when I proposed an arts section for the publication. He didn't really understand what I was aiming for, but he often seemed like he wanted to learn from me about it. He seemed earnest, in that regard. And so I thought there was still something we could gain from working together.

I didn't see too much of Yuli except when Neil and I met up with her. I could tell that she was probably more interested in hanging out with Neil — who was in comparison much more a foreigner, a strange, liminal character. By then, my Mandarin had improved a lot, but we talked in English when Neil was around. Maybe there was a part of me that resented that lack of interest in who I was. Even so, I realized that was just her character — she would always be distracted by one or another of the million other activist projects she was involved in after the end of the occupation and didn't always have time for us. Maybe I shouldn't have taken it personally, but I didn't have anyone who I was close to in those days. In the absence of anyone else I could really connect with, my best option was Neil.

There were others I had been close to in the past. Ray, for example, who I had known as a family friend. But she wasn't living in Taiwan then; she was still attending college in Chicago, and someone like David wouldn't understand what I was wrapped up in.

Seeking the same kind of intimacy I'd had with David and Aoi in New York, a part of me had hoped for a stronger relation between me, Yuli, and Neil. Was it that I was always seeking to restage the past? Trying to rewrite it according to the demands of the present? It was easier to avoid both being alone and a sense of temporal anomie by immersing myself in the vast span of human history.

We once went to the beach together. It was in Gongliao, where a nuclear plant was under construction. The Fukushima disaster in Japan had a large impact on Taiwan. There'd already been an anti-nuclear movement in past decades, but after Fukushima, there was a new wave of organizing over fears that Taiwan could see a similar disaster, as it had frequent earthquakes too, and a similar history of government mismanagement under the KMT. The reactor itself loomed over the beach, which was full of tourists. It had been covered up with a large blue tarp on one side, but the overall effect was tawdry.

Some kind of electronic music festival was underway when we arrived, and as we were to find out, the music kept blaring out into the night and people kept dancing. Neil and I chatted to some of the expats as we explored the beach, and we decided that they were "trash foreigners."

"How can you tell when someone is a trash foreigner and when someone isn't?" asked Yuli, after watching the interaction.

"If someone is only here to party and that's literally the only thing they're interested in."

"Hey, I like to party," said Neil.

"But that's not the only thing you're interested in. In life, I mean."

We bought beers from a convenience store. That night, on the beach, we drank while watching the waves. I stared at the sea and thought about how the ocean lay between me and all the places I felt connected to, the US, Japan. No man was an island, I knew — how did that quote go again? We are all linked together, as though an archipelago? I couldn't remember, not after a few beers. Even if we sought and found some emotional connection, human experience made it feel as though we were all isolated islands unto ourselves.

I voiced something to that effect aloud, probably incoherently. The other two laughed and Neil started ribbing me about how pessimistic and negative I often was. He called me a misanthrope. It was all good fun, but maybe it did say something about how my negativity tended to seep into everything I did. We had to look up the word in Chinese for Yuli. She laughed when she read the entry.

"That's you, alright."

"I mean, everyone is just pretending to be happy, right?" I said. They both looked at me quizzically. "You don't think so? Maybe you're just better at pretending than me."

We started talking about our ambitions.

Yuli wasn't happy with her current stint as a medical student and wanted to transfer to philosophy or literature. She wanted to study abroad someday, and was drawn to France specifically. Neil was thinking about graduate school or finding some kind of research position, probably with the aim of catapulting off of that to something else. As for me, I was also thinking about graduate school. I didn't inherently like academia, it just it didn't seem as though there were a lot of places in the capitalist world that would allow me to think and reflect and be able to survive in some kind of way.

The three of us still had school in mind, then. Still, there was a big difference between Yuli, Neil, and me. He and I had a way to get off the island whenever we wanted to take it, but for Yuli, or anyone else who was a citizen, it would be something she would have to fight for. Still, she was a bit younger than we were and had more time to think about the future.

Of those who had been born one generation after the KMT came to Taiwan, there was a wave that had gone abroad, usually through graduate school, and stayed there. Often, they were already part of an educational elite in Taiwan, having gone to top schools like National Taiwan University. There was a sing-song idiom from that era: "Go — go — go to National Taiwan University, go — go — go — to America." My father had graduated from National Taiwan University, then moved to New York for graduate school and never left, and so I owed my existence, really, to this uneven relationship between the US and Taiwan.

The US had long loomed over Taiwan and been idealized by generations of Taiwanese in sometimes rather utopian terms — and this despite the fact that the KMT could not have ruled over Taiwan without US backing. Even though it was only while studying in the US that many activists in the democracy movement had learned about the political killings committed by the KMT, they still tended to see the US in rosy terms. But it was also true that my own lived experience in Taiwan had become a process of unlearning things. It could be disorienting, in rather unexpected ways, unearthing unconscious associations, memories, and attachments and trying to reshape them according to the demands of the moment; even something as simple as learning that a favorite snack from my childhood — the Want Want cracker — was owned by a massive pro-China conglomerate. I had associated Want Want crackers — which came in both sweet and savory versions — with a Chinese supermarket in New Jersey that my family went to every few weeks to stock up on food. It was a favorite snack of mine after school. I would gorge myself on the crackers and lick off the remnants from my fingers greedily. This turned out to be true as well of many of my peers who'd grown up in Taiwan.

In the years prior, that conglomerate — the Want Want Group — had taken to buying up Taiwanese media companies and retooling them to censor negative coverage of China and promote positive views of the CCP. The founder was one of the richest men in Taiwan, and so, like many members of the 1 percent, it was no surprise that he was in favor of political unification — China could offer even more markets to tap into, no matter what the impact on Taiwan's political freedoms would be. The bourgeoisie the world over was all too willing to sell away the futures of young people, I knew — having gone to NYU, my peers and I all faced a lifetime of student debt, and it was no surprise that this had crystallized into something like Occupy Wall Street.

It wasn't as though the Taiwanese all thought they were Chinese and looked urgently toward the day that the mainland was taken, after all. Decades after democratization, it was only those who came to Taiwan and lorded it over others as part of the ruling elite during the authoritarian times that continued to think this. Hardly any young people had the kind of longing for China that past generations did.

No more Want Want, I declared, despite my own fond childhood memories. I didn't want to be the same as I found many from the diaspora to be: unwilling to confront and overturn their conceptions of the "sourceland" if it called into question something about their identity.

As for me, I'd never had much in the way of pride in my background holding me back anyway. Still, in this way I came to realize how much my preconceptions of Taiwan had been shaped by the things my parents told me. Equally, it was by virtue of that process of unlearning that I had been thrown into a generational movement with a group of people of roughly the same age.

That was part of growing up: coming to one's own judgments on the world, rather than just regurgitating what others told you. But there can be violence to that process, too, I now realize.

Neil came up to Taipei for a few days and I took the time to show him around. He called the Chiang Kai-shek Memorial in Taipei a "mini-Tiananmen Square."

"That's all?" said Neil once we were done looking through the memorial. "It's so *small.*"

Part of what colored his experiences of Taiwan was that he had spent some time in China before. As for me, Taiwan was simply Taiwan. My memories of Taiwan went back to childhood. As for China, it was simply a place I had been to as an adult. When I had gone before, it had just been as a vacation spot. I felt offended by Neil's comment, strangely, though I didn't say anything. But he was right. I felt it was small, too. Compared to New York, everything was small.

The difference between him and me was that I had a sense of identification with the place. He didn't.

He and I were Americans when it came down to it. The island felt pretty parochial to me sometimes, too. Yet I didn't like how he talked about Taiwan sometimes. I didn't — or I had learned not to — scoff at the lived experience of people here.

But for the people that live there, it was their lives, it was their island, it was their world. Not everyone could be privileged, cosmopolitan Americans such as us.

"It reminds me of Kyoto," I said — another place I had only fleeting experience of.

Perhaps that was a harbinger of the tensions that began to develop between us. They develop within any team, I realize, but the main source of the tensions was very specifically between Neil and me. Perhaps it was inevitable and I should have acknowledged earlier that he and I were bound for conflict.

It started with Neil not liking my articles. Part of the tension came from our different working styles. I tended to prioritize keeping the group together, even if it meant subpar content went out. Neil was more focused on quality, even if it meant friction. He started talking about cutting the sections of the publication he didn't care for, such as the Chinese section. I declared in the group chat that I would be quitting, though in reality I knew it was a hollow threat, just a way to get Neil to come to the table to talk.

After three days of confrontation, I went down to Tainan to meet him and try to work it out. Things came to a head in a conveyor-belt sushi place. The meeting was a tense one.

We argued in the midst of the cheery and bright J-pop, while slices of sushi rolls went around on conveyor belts. I was unclear why Neil had picked somewhere like this as a place to meet — it wasn't exactly the most conducive to discussion. That already put me on edge.

"I don't know what was with that piece!" Neil intoned at me. "You let us down."

"Well, I never said that I was a good writer." I sighed. The blaring Japanese pop music hurt my ears. "You don't have to have me write for this publication if you don't want to," I said. "But if you're going to complain about my articles, get me your articles *ahead* of time if you want me to edit them."

The previous week, Neil had sent me his article at 3am the morning it was supposed to go online, and I wasn't happy about having to edit an article at the very last minute. The publication wasn't going the way I imagined it at all, but I had to ask myself what in fact I had imagined. In retrospect, maybe I could have been more honest about my stake in the whole matter; after all, the publication hadn't been *my* idea.

"I don't really have to write for this publication at all," I reiterated. "We have enough English editors. Cheng can just take over for me."

"There's no running this publication without you. You know it, too," said Neil. It was true, at that point I bottom-lined too many things for *Daybreak* to keep running if I wasn't around. Maybe that had been my way of making sure that I couldn't easily be disposed of.

"So, my condition for staying on is that the Chinese-language section remains."

Neil hadn't really seen any point in having a Chinese-language section, while, for me, there didn't seem to be any way of making inroads or creating dialogue between Taiwan and the wider world without the publication being bilingual. After all, publications like *Daybreak* were pretty commonplace. What was less common, what I didn't really see any other publications doing at the time, was attempting to have exchanges between Chinese and English.

My aim with *Daybreak* was to have a publication in which Taiwanese could speak on their own behalf in the international sphere. But sometimes they seemed fine with others speaking for them. Usually white people. It bothered me. But sometimes the assumption seemed to be that others would be better at expressing Taiwan's situation than Taiwanese themselves.

Maybe we all had our insecurities, and perhaps Taiwan's international exclusion had left it desperate for attention from the outside world. I tended to see that a lot in how the Taiwanese interacted with expats — and maybe that's how they regarded me as well. I could never be so sure. I didn't think the Taiwanese could really depend on anyone but themselves, frankly. Yet sometimes there was no way to explain all this without coming across as insulting or condescending. Maybe it all went back to the strange forgetfulness that let the Taiwanese believe the US might save them, even though they backed the KMT.

"So, you stay on as the managing editor. But you don't write."

I shrugged. I came to feel differently later on, but at that time I never thought I had any real contributions to make to whatever could be said about Taiwan, whether in English or Chinese.

"You're just so damned passive," said Neil. I felt a sudden surge of anger, then I calmed myself.

"I put the team before myself," I said.

"Don't act so self-righteous."

I shrugged again. A part of me felt that he was accusing me of being passive because I was Asian. A part of me hated that I was falling back on arguments about putting the group before myself, as though this argument reflected some kind of stereotyped binary between Asian collectivism and Western individualism.

"I just don't get where this is all coming from," Neil said. "You get so… defensive."

"I'm part of this publication because Taiwan needs a voice. That's all."

"You don't have any ambition." said Neil.

"Maybe I don't."

For some time, I had been feeling pretty alienated from my fellow Americans. I realized that in all my years of wandering, there were things in Taiwan I had never seen anywhere else. I had never seen the coming together of art and social activism the way I had here. I had never seen that many young people interested in politics.

I don't think it was the fact that I was "from" here in some sense which led to that perception, but I realized Neil wouldn't get it. Taiwan. China. Asia. These were all just places he was passing through, but as for me, I had spent enough time wandering and there had come point at which I needed to find a place to take a stand.

So, it was then I realized I couldn't, in fact, simply sit back and let *Daybreak* be a publication controlled by Americans.

"That's just your version of the story," said Yuli when I told all this to her once I was back in Taipei. We were in another activist coffee shop, near the rear gate of National Taiwan University. "I don't see what you're talking about at all. You just have a really negative read on Neil. I don't know who to believe."

"I know I'm right about Neil," I said. I had told her that my suspicion was that he eventually hoped to use the publication as some career credit to get to China. It came up in conversation too often, the way he viewed Taiwan as some kind of alternative version of China. Sooner or later, he would want to get to the real deal.

"You said once to me that you were always just splitting up with people every few years. That you had just been drifting from place to place because you were always feeling alienated from them and lashing out at them. Isn't that what's happening again?"

"What do you want me to do to prove it? Make a recording of one of our conversations?" I laughed somewhat bitterly. "The way he talks to me about these things is different than how he'd be willing to talk to you about it. We're Americans, after all. That's about it."

Yuli sighed. She had realized early on that I was a deeply untrusting individual, even a paranoid one. It was true.

"Why are you taking this so personally?" she asked. "Why is this so serious to you?"

Why indeed? It was a matter of identity, I suppose. I had never particularly been interested in Asian culture or history or anything like that growing up. I hung out with the white kids, like David, primarily. The other Asians liked to call me a banana — yellow on the outside, but white on the inside. But I had felt that all the Asian kids just stuck together out of some sort of herd mentality. Insofar as they felt insecure in a white-dominant society, clinging to cultural identity felt like a sort of safety blanket to me, and I was always questioning how Asian they really were when their knowledge of Asia often seemed to go little further than fortune cookies and zodiac signs.

For a moment I felt almost cosmically alone, caught in the gravitational pull of *the emptiness*, with nothing to follow but your voice, V, in the distance of eternity. I wasn't Chinese or Chinese American, though I had thought otherwise for years because of my KMT background. I wasn't Taiwanese either, since I hadn't grown up in Taiwan. I was just an American. But with Americans, there was always the fact that I wasn't a white American. There would always be certain expectations of me as an Asian person. Sometimes, with people I had grown up with, like David, I would forget that I was different from them — for a little while at least. But then it would suddenly be all too apparent again.

Even when the Taiwanese told me that I was one of them, I could tell that nobody really thought so. I looked different, I carried myself differently, and my accent was off. Well, they were right, so I didn't blame them. What I couldn't stand above all else was when someone made a big show of me being Taiwanese, saying that I had done so much for Taiwan through participating in the Sunflower Movement or starting

Daybreak or what have you. When someone told me that, in their eyes, I knew more about Taiwan than many Taiwanese did, I could see that they still thought of me as an interloper.

Taiwanese Americans by and large didn't understand me either. Matters of identity were often an ingrained emotional reaction for them, even when this just disguised how shallow their understanding of Taiwan was — or that their idea of Taiwan was just something they themselves had imagined into being. Taiwanese Americans or other Asian Americans often clung to an imagined version of their roots in order to deal with their sense of not belonging to white American society. A coping mechanism. I couldn't abide by that.

In my head, I started dividing up the group into people who would side with Neil and those who would side with me. Maybe it was paranoia, but I was convinced that most of the group would, by default, side with Neil.

I did question myself regarding how I felt about Neil, and a part of me realized I was probably projecting the specter of David — or of other white people in my life — onto him. Was I really that sensitive to white people? Maybe I wasn't so different than all of those Asian kids I had grown up with after all.

I knew that Neil wasn't David. He was ambitious in a way that David wasn't, obviously. But despite being quite different, I increasingly found that I saw them the same way. They triggered the same anxieties, perhaps.

"Why are you taking this so personally?" Yuli asked again.

Why indeed? But why was Yuli involved in all this, anyway?

In her case, a large part of her interest in the project was likely based on the participation of a high number of foreigners, and this was probably the reason she had kept up contact with me in the beginning, too, since I was also an odd foreigner.

I didn't blame her. I myself sometimes wondered whether I found Taiwan to be so fascinating due to projections of my own. Whether it was Yuli or me, for some people it's impossible not to be drawn toward what is different or exotic. It was rather like that with Aoi, too, for that matter. Was I in any position to judge Aoi or Yuli? People who, unlike me, were not Westerners?

Yuli could be difficult to deal with. I was still a bit hurt by the fact that she had just ignored me while in the Legislative Yuan, not responding to any of my messages asking her if she was alright.

She seemed to have forgotten about everything else in her life then, whether it was me, her other friends, her parents, or anything else.

A few months prior, during the legislative occupation, her parents had actually travelled from Chiayi to Taipei to look for her, since she had gone against their wishes in participating in the movement and they were worried. It was kind of sweet, thinking about it. But, since then, relations had been tense with her folks. Yuli had stayed for a while with her sister in Kaohsiung after the occupation, to get away from them, before moving back to Taipei.

Still, she had an idealism that I admired along with her headstrong nature. On the night of 318, she had been on the front lines of the protest, screaming at police. I saw her on the cover of the *Apple Daily* that day. There was a reason she had the fire to stand up and fight that night in March, or on the many nights after. I suspect she had what I precisely lacked — a genuine sense of political commitment to a cause. A willingness to risk it all. I certainly hadn't been like that when I was nineteen. I was already quite cynical even then. Maybe that's what drew me to the young people of Taiwan. A sense that they had something which I had long since lost. Or which I'd perhaps never had.

Maybe I just envied her sense of courage because I, by contrast, was just a coward. I had never been willing to take such risks for things I believed in. In all likelihood, I just didn't believe in anything strongly enough, and I couldn't see myself ever believing in anything that strongly, in spite of the values and ideals I otherwise professed to. I could only see myself in my own narrow slice of reality for the rest of time. It made me feel a sense of shame in how lowly I was as a person who claimed to have political commitments. Funny how things would change later, in just the space of a few short years.

Yuli might have come to despise me in the end. Why had I made things so complicated anyway? And because I opened up to her about my anxieties, she eventually stopped talking to me. I was always alienating people or pushing them away. It was just too much a part of me.

It's only you who has never left me, V. You at least, who I have never been able to escape.

On one of the last nights that Neil was in Taiwan, we got drinks. He was moving to Beijing, having picked up a position there. The truth was that I planned to leave soon as well, having been accepted to an MA program at Columbia.

We sat on the floor of Zhexiong's apartment, all of us, the *Daybreak* crew, smoking and drinking Taiwan Beer. I was feeling irritated and slightly drunk. "What do you know about activism, anyway? This is all just some damn adventure for you," I said to Neil.

Suddenly everyone was staring. Neil raised an eyebrow but was quiet. "Chill."

"Did you ever actually care about any of the things you claimed to care about? I doubt you actually did."

"Somebody needs to chill the fuck out," said Neil.

"You've been having a good fucking time here, haven't you?" I spat out. "*Why did you ever come here?*"

Over the past month, I had come to gradually feel rather disgusted with Neil. Bumbling around, always the loud obnoxious American. People seemed to like him, though. He could be charming. And they were enthralled by the fact that he was a foreigner.

"Why shouldn't I have come here?" asked Neil, suddenly rather cold. "I found what was going on here *interesting*. So I came here."

"You don't even have a stake in any of this," I said. "You can always run back to America at any time." As I said this, I thought about how the same was true for me.

"It's inspiring. That young people here are struggling for what they believe in."

"You're such a fucking *American*," I responded. It all just sounded like some bullshit from something out of a social studies textbook.

"But aren't you as well?"

Coming from him, that was just too much. And then, suddenly, I was at him. I caught him once on the jaw with my fist, then again as I knocked him onto the floor. A bottle on the table near us fell and shattered. Someone pulled me off of him. He wasn't hurt, but he seemed appalled. That look of shock on his face — it was so *satisfying*! I laughed.

I had too much damned venom coursing through my veins. I often thought that I was toxic. And there was a part of me with an urge to inflict pain on others. But wasn't a little venom justified? A part of me still thinks so. Another part of me realizes that I acted out of *fear*. I was unable to overcome my own fear, my own resentment. That wasn't the only possible outcome. Violence was about the only thing that made me feel alive sometimes. Inflicting it on other people. Having it inflicted on me. I had done my fair share of both.

Neil went back to America the next morning. I never really spoke to him again, at least not directly. He eventually dropped out of the publication when he couldn't keep up the workload. I suspect that he had gone in with unrealistic expectations of what it took to run something like *Daybreak* to begin with. But maybe it wouldn't have ended the way it did if I had been a bit more honest from the beginning.

Yuli drifted out of *Daybreak* as well. I would run into her whenever I was back in Taiwan at what used to be our usual spots in Taipei, but I never talked to her. It had become too uncomfortable since she had become caught between Neil and me. The rest of us never spoke of that abortive confrontation again.

I asked Ray to join *Daybreak* soon after, since we needed more people and I needed someone I could rely on consistently. Part of my decision was probably informed by the fact that she had a similar sense of identity to me. I wouldn't make the same mistake again. Of the three people who began *Daybreak* — Neil, Yuli, and me — I was the only one left. I was always the last man standing in the wreckage of anything I involved myself in.

Daybreak took off pretty quickly after that. I was right about there being a real vacuum in Taiwan for something like it. After a year, there were fifteen people: Jack, a Taiwanese Trotskyist living in New York City; Eliot, a photographer of social movements; Paul and Toby, who were both translators; and many others. I loved the sense of camaraderie. Those were still times we felt to be revolutionary, and that came out in the way we worked with one another. Sometimes I would wake up to find that there were already several hundred unread messages in our internal chatroom. It made it difficult to keep up sometimes, even for me, but it was a sign of how passionate we were about the things we cared for. It was a sign of authenticity.

For a moment — and just for a moment — V, I thought it all proved that I could escape the emptiness.

I moved back to New York for graduate school. It was strange that a year of life in which so much had happened could simply be packed up in a series of boxes. I had a small gathering with friends and then took the plane, I didn't want to make a big deal out of it. I knew that I would be returning someday.

I still produced the most articles for *Daybreak*, since I wrote the fastest and had the most time to spend on it. I found myself in a few tiffs with Left pro-unification types in Taiwan: Taiwanese leftists who idealized China as some kind of socialist utopia — oftentimes it went back to the fact that, like me, they were mainlanders and still felt some kind of cultural attachment to China. I felt sometimes I was being set up to go after them by others who had something to lose in attacking them head-on in terms of their careers. As for me, I had nothing to lose, so I could go after them with abandon. I acquired a reputation for intellectual aggressiveness that way. It was all the same to me. Sometimes I wasn't really sure why I felt compelled to attack someone. But all that venom needed to go somewhere. At least, this way, it could be put to some productive use.

Negativity. *Destroying* other people. I knew that there was an inner violence to me that wouldn't go away anytime soon; that seemed to be the pattern — better it be turned toward those who would hurt me or those I loved than that I end up taking it out on those I cared for the most. Even then, I wasn't sure any of this accomplished anything. But I put up a pretty good show of acting as though I did. That was the way to keep the publication together: acting as though I bought into something. It was like Pascal's wager or Kierkegaard's leap of faith. And I was a pretty good actor, at that.

A part of me questioned whether we were simply getting places because there was a lack of people doing the same thing in Taiwan. There was a relative paucity of English-language content. We weren't necessarily the best and brightest, after all, and our success was probably down to it being a small island and there being nobody else. Between life as a grad student at Columbia during the day and all the time I spent writing articles for *Daybreak* at night, my life was taken up with words, but then perhaps the world exists in order to be made into a book, as Mallarmé said. In a way, I felt I needed to just keep writing, otherwise I would drown under the weight of my own self-doubt. I did not identify as Taiwanese or American but with the space, the literal space, between the two words on a printed page. I was constituted by that emptiness.

I was in America *and* Taiwan, with my life divided into two camps, but whether those I encountered or worked alongside were Taiwanese, Chinese, American, Taiwanese American, or Chinese American, I felt that my own sense of identification — or maybe my lack thereof — meant that nobody could understand me. I was an orphan of Asia and America. I was an orphan of the world, it seemed.

But did it matter? The strong should learn to be lonely. That's what I've learned. Someone once commented to me that my Mandarin didn't sound like the Mandarin of a non-native speaker. Not like a Taiwanese or Chinese person's Mandarin, but not like a non-native speaker either. I guess that's what it was. I was the native speaker of a language from a place that didn't exist, of which I was the only citizen.

Or perhaps I'm not the only one — you, too, speak this language of mine, this idiolect, don't you, V.

It isn't so easy to kill God and storm heaven, you know? However many books you've read, they won't help with that. It is only now, looking back and putting together the pieces, that I realize this was the second time I died. Any occupation ends, sooner or later, with an eviction, and perhaps there's a part of me that has always been seeking absolution at the end of a police officer's truncheon. Death for a cause would have meant some kind of commitment, right, V? Sometimes I still think about that rush charging the Executive Yuan. Because there were a number of possible futures, fates, outcomes, that could have resulted that day. One of those was death. Another missed opportunity then. I didn't manage the death I would have wanted. Or perhaps the death I wanted really was always at your hands, V.

In the end, I will just be a corpse, like all the rest. Of course, in a way I had always been a living corpse, but there are some moments when the internal rot shows through quite clearly. When the sun rises, at daybreak, there's no hiding your own decay.

Part 3

By the summer of 2015, I was back in Taiwan and living in a small run-down room on Siwei Road in Daan. Although in the same upscale part of town, the apartment I lived in seemed like it was close to a hundred years old. It was infested with ants, and parts of the roof leaked when it rained, which was quite often. There was no air conditioning, so it was always hot.

The apartment belonged to a friend of my mother who was renting me the place for the summer at a discount. I had four other roommates, but because of the strange hours I kept and the fact that their doors were always closed and there was no kitchen or shared common area, I never saw any of them during the several months I spent there. I knew that most of them were women. The only indicator that there was another man living there was that the seat was sometimes left up on the toilet in the communal bathroom. It felt like living with a group of ghosts.

Sometimes in the afternoons, when work permitted, I would get coffee with Ray. We had known each other since we were kids, from summers in Taipei, because our parents were friends. There weren't a lot of people like us. That we were both Taiwanese but grew up mostly abroad was one reason why we became friends. We had both spent our formative years outside of Taiwan, to be sure, but we both thought of ourselves as Taiwanese in some way. Otherwise, we wouldn't be here. I knew I could trust her perspective. It was why I had asked her to be an editor on *Daybreak* shortly after we started the publication.

Ray had spent much longer in Taiwan than I had. She had even been one of the Wild Strawberries in 2008, occupying Liberty Square at the start of the Ma administration. She probably understood the dynamics of how the cops behaved there better than I did, but I had more experience with social movements on the whole. It was useful having a colleague with a complementary skillset in this way.

Ray and I lived near each other. Her apartment was on the other side of the roundabout where Ren'ai Road met Dunhua South Road, diagonal from my apartment. We would meet up and work in the coffee/record shop in the Eslite basement. We would browse the books in the actual bookstore on the second floor when we got bored, and then eat and drink in one of the small restaurants and bars in the narrow alleys around her place or mine. We'd complain about our love lives, gossip, and talk about activist politics.

I enjoyed those days with Ray, sitting and working together quietly and methodically. It reminded me of the hours spent with Aoi and David in coffee shops in New York City, back before it all went wrong between us — just sitting and talking as we navigated our daily affairs as students.

Did that mean I had grown nostalgic? Certainly I had been going over the past a lot lately. Were the "me" that had been in New York and the "me" that was in Taipei the same person at the end of the day? I was still brooding over the nature of belief — what did it mean to believe something strongly enough to stake your life on it? David's observation back in Tokyo, that the "self" you are in different cities of the world isn't the same person, had stuck with me. I thought about Aoi too, and wondered again if I was really so different to her. I, too, was a fanatic. Do real fanatics question themselves? Ask whether they are, in fact, fanatical? I'm pretty sure that they do. And V, we are both seeking the unrealized promises of our past in our future, are we not? Is that not fanaticism in its truest sense?

July 30, the day the occupation started, was another scorching afternoon, but surprisingly enough, it didn't rain. In summer in Taipei, it rains nearly every afternoon due to the city being located in a basin and because of the oppressive humidity. Ray wasn't doing too well. She had gone through a breakup with her girlfriend the previous month, and shortly after became smitten with a girl who was probably straight. Ray had long had the habit of falling in love too easily.

"Aren't you a bit old to be falling for straight girls?" We were in a coffee shop by Gongguan that doubled as a venue called Kafka on the Shore, named after the Murakami novel; perhaps it was this, too, that had set me off thinking about David and Aoi. It played tasteful music, the air conditioning was strong, it was open late, and, most importantly, it served alcohol and was good for a drink once you were done with the coffee.

"I know, but it felt like… destiny. Like I had known her before from somewhere." She had met the girl at a conference for a Taiwanese student organization we *Daybreak* folk were all involved in.

I shrugged. "You can't always trust your feelings."

"I know, I know…"

I thought about how to put what I was thinking into words for a few moments, then gave up.

I took a sip of coffee. I myself had a strong sense of predestination. I didn't believe in the human soul, life after death, or any form of existence preceding birth, but I had often felt as though all my actions were just repeating something I had done before, or that I was living out the consequences of a previous life.

"So how about you? How are things with Xixi?" she asked. Xixi was my girlfriend at the time, a Chinese student in the same department as me at Columbia. She was in Beijing, working a summer gig teaching Chinese to American students. We had started dating several months prior, before I had returned to Taiwan and she to China for the summer.

"Same old, same old. But she's having visa issues getting back to the US. Makes me a bit worried."

Daybreak wasn't on the radar of the Chinese government yet, but it was only a matter of time, and I worried that my work would affect her. Whenever I made plans to go to China, I was never sure if I would be able to get in — and if I did, whether I would be able to get out again. Those were the years before Taiwanese started to be kidnapped in China, and before the worst of it began, but even then I was cautious about what could happen to her because of me, and I thought, not for the first time, that once China invaded, I would end up getting shot in a concentration camp.

Ray had to get back to work, so I went wandering, browsing the bookstores and peering into the narrow alleyways around National Taiwan University. You never knew what you would find between the old, decaying buildings and all the new high-rises coming up. The old was being devoured, and it didn't matter much what was uprooted — or who. After a few hours it started raining. It was always raining, but that still couldn't wash away the bloodstains, which were everywhere if you looked hard enough. I liked to walk around the alleyways and imagine the time before I had been born. A flaneur among the bloodstains.

Decades on from the White Terror, it sometimes wasn't so easy to call Taiwan a democracy, I thought. The criminals of the past, people who had blood on their hands from that era, were often still active figures in public life. Some remained part of the government. The history was still all quite fresh — and not safely dead yet. Look closely enough and any street corner in the city might have been the site of some execution a few decades back.

That Taiwan was said to have already gone through democratization and reform made it easier for them to get away from their past crimes, since now they could claim that the sins of the past were just long-dead history. When former victims of the authoritarian period demanded justice, the KMT could even claim that *they* were the ones now out for political revenge, that *they* were the ones stirring up the old hatreds of the past. I found it to be a rather thin pretense for claiming that the problems of the past had all been worked through and no longer mattered.

Still, just as there was a history of bloodshed, there was also a history of resistance. In that respect, I was also often surprised at the history in plain sight. Even the bookstores around National Taiwan University had sold banned books during the authoritarian period.

When talking to anyone from that period, you never knew who could have been a collaborator or part of the resistance.

But sometimes that all made me wonder if my involvement in Taiwanese politics was because I was descended from members of the KMT. This is to say, was I motivated by guilt? The visceral thrill that came with the rush of adrenaline from facing down the riot police — was that how I hoped for absolution?

Eventually I tired of my wanderings. I went back to my place, finished writing an article, and lay down in the early evening to rest.

There I am, on my mattress on the floor in the sticky evening heat. I close my eyes and remember that you told me once of your premonition, V. That sooner or later, one of us would have to die before the other. We had told the other that whichever one of us fell would have to crawl over the other's corpse. The quickest way was for one of us to kill the other. That was the only way any of us could have a future, right? You're either the executioner or the executed; that was simply life, was it not? Well, I had started to become haunted by that thought as well. But perhaps if yours was the power of foresight and the gaze into the wreckage of the future, what I had was a gaze into the unrealized possibilities of the past.

But I'm tired of it now. There had to be a way out. I refused to believe that eternity was only the aggregation of all these days of trying to kill the self of one day prior, of attempting to kill one's future self, or that one of us would have to kill the other and that was simply fate. And maybe the way out was *the emptiness*. The absence of possibility was also the possibility of possibility, was it not?

Every person I knew was always the memory of a memory of a memory. When you meet someone new, you only know them in terms of the people you knew in the past, and that's how they know you. When you go somewhere new, it's just the memory of a place written on your memory of a previous place. Haunted by thought, I snapped to wakefulness. I could feel someone crying out to me.

I had been woken by a call on my cell. It was Ray again. It was shortly after 10pm.

"Q.Q., where the fuck are you? You haven't been keeping track of the news."

I sat up from the mattress. I had fallen asleep with the radio on. The noise of static was interspersed with the programming — something about the strength of the typhoon approaching Taiwan. I glanced out the window. The night was dark, and I was sweating. Sometimes it felt like all I did was read and write, trapped in an endless cycle of devouring and regurgitating words.

"You've got to get to the Ministry of Education."

"What happened?" I asked. "Another demonstration?"

"A student killed himself this morning. Ryo Lin. They're having a memorial ceremony for him at the Ministry of Education."

"You think it'll turn into something?"

"It's not impossible."

"Okay, I'm there." I threw on a pair of sneakers — in case I would have to run from the police that night — locked the door, and flagged down a taxi on the street outside. I made small talk with the driver while checking Facebook to see which groups were on site. It was all the usual suspects. He asked me what I did, and I told him: journalist.

In the beginning, I just called myself a journalist and showed up at press conferences as though I was supposed to be there. Eventually, as people began to read what I wrote, other people started calling me a journalist too. That's how I entered the profession. But that wasn't unusual at a time when there were all these new outlets, citizen journalist initiatives, that had emerged in the wake of the Sunflower Movement.

"Don't forget!" the taxi driver gestured to his neck as I got out. "The police," he said by way of explanation. He was reminding me not to forget my press pass. Evidently, he had driven journalists before.

There were a lot of kids outside of the Ministry of Education, all high school students, and I felt an immediate sense of identification, though another part of me wondered sometimes if I was just clinging to my fading youth through my interest in the idealism of high schoolers.

Ryo Lin had killed himself that morning by charcoal poisoning. A little less than a week before, on July 23, he had been among a group of students who had charged and attempted to occupy the Ministry of Education. The central issue had been textbook changes that tried to depict Taiwan as having always been part of China — changes that were being pushed for by the KMT. Any history which suggested that Taiwan was not part of China, the KMT tried to bury.

There's always an awkwardness and a tension to any kind of protest. So many people standing there, milling about. They might be chatting with their friends or acquaintances, or just taking in their surroundings. This was the case that night, too. But the air was heavier than usual — the sense of grief was palpable.

"You don't think the Grey Wolf will turn up, do you?" Ray asked me quietly.

Sometimes I still thought about the incident when he had shown up to the legislature last year — a strange day of watching the police do nothing as literal gangsters responsible for political killings in decades past faced down student demonstrators. You didn't see as much of that in post-authoritarian times, but I knew that it was the norm for those who had been involved in protest before, during the White Terror.

"He would know how bad it would look, even for him. I mean, someone died, didn't they?" I muttered. "What, did you hear something?"

She shrugged. Those were the years in which any protest could potentially turn violent, after all. I turned my attention back to the gathering crowd and the swelling tension.

"You think something will happen tonight?" asked Ray.

It was my turn to shrug. "If after someone dies, nothing happens, then it's over."

I had been monitoring the textbook issue for some time; there had been a failed attempt a few months prior in March by around two hundred demonstrators to reoccupy the Legislative Yuan during the one-year anniversary of the Sunflower Movement. About thirty people had been arrested, mostly students. But since then, there had been a strange quiescence around the issue, with seemingly no one able to rally any action. I had been there that night, right by the front lines of those attempting to force their way into the building, but other than that there hadn't been major actions other than fleeting street demonstrations.

It was an attempt to replicate the movement by carrying out the same set of actions from a year prior. It reminded me of the many attempts to occupy Zuccotti Park again that I had seen in the wake of Occupy Wall Street, or the way that the post-Fukushima protests in some way replayed the 1960s and '70s in variation. In those cases, I wasn't convinced that carrying out the same set of actions would have a better outcome. But sometimes that's trauma, isn't it? Movements have many afterlives. And there was always the question of why I was there participating in these compulsive repetitions, too.

That I'd attended the March protest meant I had been in the same space as Ryo Lin, however briefly. At twenty-three, I wasn't even much older than he was. He had also been part of the abortive charge, and now he was dead. Sometime before he committed suicide, he had said that he would do something that would give new life to the movement. Had he hoped to create that new life by taking his own?

His boyfriend gave a speech. The high schoolers lit candles and burnt ghost money. Pictures of the Minister of Education had been stuck to the looming, eight-foot-tall black barriers which had been erected outside the Ministry of Education by police the week before. The word "Murderer" was written on them. Razor wire, with barbs the size of X-Acto blades, was draped around the barriers. The only lighting came from dim streetlamps, and the long shadows of the razor wire strewn along the barriers stretched out into the distance.

It would have been Lin's twentieth birthday that day. Who knows? It's possible that he had decided to die that day deliberately. Maybe he also had the same fear as I do: of getting older, of spending the rest of one's life pursuing the diminishing echoes of past moments that seemed as though they could be redemptive of all that came before. Maybe some years down the line, perhaps decades from now, it will be me fleeing into the subways with aged comrades — older and wearier each year, while the police continued to be ever youthful. Time goes on, you get older, the world still refuses to change.

Candles were distributed among the gathered. Someone led the crowd in singing "Happy Birthday." Some were in tears. As for me, I couldn't stop thinking about how hot and sticky the night was. These were the kind of nights when you knew anything could happen. The summer night feels immanent with possibility sometimes. No doubt about it, something would happen. I could feel it in my bones. Perhaps the Grey Wolf would arrive after all. "Perhaps you'll get your chance," *the emptiness* said to me.

"What does that mean?" I asked out loud, then, as another protester glanced at me, I looked at my phone to avoid their gaze. I had a text from Xixi. Had something happened to her? No, why would she be at risk? It was me that was in the thick of it all; but still, the fact that she was so far away was unsettling no matter how instantaneous communication between us could be. It was just a message to see how I was and what I was doing. I replied with something bland and general, cautious about sharing information about what I was up to over the internet. Who knew whether it could all be later weaponized against her in some form?

Sometime later, Ray found me again, having drifted away to take some photos. The crowd had increased in number by then. News reports started coming in that several individuals had tried to charge the Legislative Yuan. We walked over and found that a small crowd had gathered outside already. Despite the massive fortifications around the Ministry of Education nearby, the legislature had minimal security, and it looked as though several people had gotten in then slipped out again. Eventually, someone with a loud voice took charge and got the crowd to go back to the Ministry of Education.

The police tended to wait until after midnight, when the trains stopped running, before taking any action to clear the streets. That way, fewer people would come in response to any police action.

Nonetheless, it was after midnight when the charge into the Ministry of Education began.

Two months before that, on a warm May day in New York City, not too long after we started dating, Xixi had asked me, "Why do you care so strongly about all these movements? Is it your background?" She meant this as a friendly query, but I could detect some anxiety.

We were sitting in her apartment in Harlem, a large complex where a number of Chinese students lived. She told me that some of the other Chinese students were afraid to venture north of the 135th Street station. I had found that amusing.

We were sharing a beer. Tsingtao. It was late afternoon. I didn't normally drink during the daytime, but she insisted. It seemed like something she expected me to do. We were chatting about my politics. My views on Taiwan's sovereignty were well known among the Chinese students, but I realized it made me interesting to them — that, as well as being a Taiwanese American who was able to speak in Mandarin. I wasn't the only diaspora person in the program, but the rest didn't seem to have the same language skills. It also surprised me to learn that there weren't actually a lot of Asian Americans or members of the diaspora studying Asia, they seemed to prefer topics like American Studies or Cultural Studies.

A part of me was surprised to have ended up back in New York City, but another part of me already knew that I would return again and again, then leave. Perhaps for the thrill of it.

Or perhaps simply because everywhere started to bore me if I lived there long enough.

I had met Xixi because I had come back to New York City, and perhaps I entered into relationships for the same reasons. That is, maybe I entered them not because I wanted to be with someone but because I wanted to hold open the possibility of leaving them. And yet, the freedom of being able to run, too, terrified me. Sometimes I just found myself in another relationship as a way out of the previous one. You are the one who will finally deliver me from the cycle, aren't you, V?

"It's a long story," I said, laying my hands flat on the table in Xixi's room. *All that history you hadn't experienced yourself and that felt like one long nightmare — and yet you existed precisely because of it,* I thought to myself. "It's part and parcel of being a leftist," I said to her.

"Being a leftist — there are a lot of people who say that they're leftists around me. I mean, I'm Chinese." She snorted.

"By that, do they just mean nationalist?"

"You see yourself as Taiwanese," Xixi said. "Not Chinese."

"Does that bother you?" I asked.

"Not really," she responded. I felt it was a bit ironic to be talking about Taiwan with alcohol from a beer named after one of China's port cities coursing through my bloodstream.

But it did bother me. Taiwan was always overshadowed, whether by China or the US. It reminded me of my own trajectory in life in some way; a life in the shadow of something I could feel but couldn't exactly see. In the era of neoliberal capitalism, with the free market's erosion of national borders, KMT elites had no real loyalty to Taiwan or the Republic of China. On the contrary, having identified with China and likely only ever seen Taiwan as a temporary colonial holding, KMT elites were probably fine with selling out to China if it was in their personal interest.

I thought I knew that myself. I mean, I was descended from them, wasn't I? I was different to a lot of other Taiwanese Americans, who took pride in their heritage, particularly if they were descended from those who had been on the political blacklist. As for me, my grandfather had been one of Chiang's direct associates. I could list his crimes. Not much to be proud of there. Perhaps it was his long shadow that I was struggling toward the light under.

"Perhaps you should be punished for his crime," *the emptiness* said to me.

I took another gulp of beer.

When the charge happened, I actually thought it was a bit farcical, but sometimes it's through farce that history gets made.

At 1:30am, a man with a megaphone announced that the action would begin, and charged, quite alone, at the barricades around the Ministry of Education. He began rattling at them and pushing them with both hands; others followed, and a ring of people with cameras gathered around them, snapping away. Most of them didn't even seem to be journalists, just people who had brought cameras hoping to get shots of the action.「湊熱鬧」, as we say in Mandarin. After something like fifteen minutes, the gates started to give way.

"Do we join in?" I asked Ray. We had been up front, but when they started pushing we had gone off to the side. She gave me a look.

"We're the press," she said. We hadn't been the year prior — we had been protesters just like them — but I guess we were now.

"The police are holding back tonight," I noted. "I thought they'd take a firmer line after last year."

"It's because the current mayor is Ko P," said Ray. "If the last guy were still mayor, it wouldn't be like this."

"We'll see," I said.

The barriers partially gave way under the pressure of the crowd, and people began covering up the razor wire with cardboard to keep from getting cut as they climbed over. I don't know where the cardboard came from. Maybe from boxes that had been brought on-site for supplies. Plastic stools had been produced from somewhere as well. This often seems to be how it is with occupations — all this stuff just appears, seemingly out of nowhere. About half the crowd clambered over into the parking lot this way. We stayed on the perimeters outside. Less than a year ago, I would have been charging in with them. Now I felt an odd sense of distance.

In the midst of occupations, I was always impressed by how quickly some people thought of what should be done — and by how well prepared some people just seem to be. Someone had the bright idea to hook up megaphones inside and outside the parking lot to allow for more coordination. Ray and I watched as one of the protesters strung up wire and a megaphone onto a tree. Eventually, after some minutes of struggling, they got it working and the crowd started using it for chants and even found someone to play the guitar and provide the crowd with music in the night. The police tried to interrupt with their own megaphone several times, but whenever they did, they were shouted down. The response was quick, rhythmic.

Time passed. The crowd forced open a side gate that allowed for free movement between the inside and outside, and as there was suddenly a lot of talk both online and within the crowd about a concerted effort by police to drive us out in the next hour, we all surged in.

I spotted a lot of familiar faces. Some of them I knew, but others were just people I had seen at protests. After Occupy Wall Street, I found that when walking around the streets of New York City, there would be a lot of faces I knew, but that they weren't people I had ever interacted with personally. Activism was always an undercurrent in any major urban center. In the months after the Sunflower Movement, I could take the metro and quickly spot who was an activist — you would see ribbons or patches on their bags, or they might be wearing black shirts, the color of the movement, with protest slogans, like "Fuck the Government" or "I don't need sex, since the government fucks me every day." If you walked into any hipster coffee shop, you would see a bunch of stickers on laptops.

My phone rang several times as people who had seen my status updates on Facebook started coming in: people arrived from an anarchist commune in Taoyuan, and from the activist group based out of Yang-Ming University that I had been so involved with the year before; there was even somebody who jumped on a high-speed train from Tainan as soon as he heard about the occupation. The nice thing about Taiwan is that when there's a protest, it's relatively easy to get to there — the island is small enough that it never takes more than a day to travel anywhere. That's probably one of the reasons why I had been so fixated on Taiwan, while Neil had just moved on — I could see something that he couldn't, something that Taiwan had that America didn't: the possibility for something close-knit and enduring to be created. And it seemed to me ironic that most Taiwanese Americans just came for a few years, found themselves unable to fit in, and then left. This was what it was for an entire generation of young people to come together in a shared collective experience and be changed by it forever — a sense of a shared mission or destiny — something I hadn't experienced elsewhere.

It was like 318 again. I guess I felt a bit happy at that. To be on the streets with a group of people you'd never thought you'd be on the streets with again, all at once — even if you didn't know all of them and never would. It's a nice feeling. Still, I couldn't help but wonder: Did I just want a replay of the past rather than something that would lead to genuine political change? The previous action hadn't been successful in fundamentally changing things either. Or did I just enjoy the sense of connection? This was what gave me a sense of being *rooted* in something, wasn't it? The sense of being physically together on the streets.

We were all grouped in the parking lot of the Ministry of Education. The area began to fill with cigarette smoke, and I spotted Chen Wei-ting, one of the leaders from the Sunflower Movement, off to the side. He seemed to be trying to stay out of the spotlight given the sexual harassment scandal that had faced him in the aftermath of the movement. I nodded at him when I passed by, and though he didn't know me, he nodded back. He seemed somewhat surprised when I stared. Why would I not?

I liked to think of those visceral moments in occupation spaces as representing the only form of genuine human connection. But not everyone was there for the same reasons. I realized that there was a lot of adolescent turmoil that went into it. Relationships. Sexuality. Loneliness, physical and emotional. That was also part of it. There were also people who simply sought power, in whatever form that took. Was it any surprise this could lead to acts of violence?

Nobody had gotten into the Ministry of Education building itself because of the riot police stationed within. At one point, I noticed that the window to the building was open; I thought of shouting out to attract the attention of the demonstrators, but questioned whether that would be unbecoming of a journalist who was no longer a protestor. Before I could react, a few moments later a security guard inside shut and locked it. It was unclear whether the occupation would last. But nobody wanted to fall back. And just like with the window, you only ever get one shot at this kind of thing — history. That's how it felt to us in the years after 2014. The future was in our hands. Or maybe another way of putting it was that we had this real sense in those years that if we screwed it up, Taiwan might not have a future.

It was probably easier to mount an occupation in Taipei than in a lot of other cities. For one, the convenience stores made it easy to stock up and resupply: though there weren't any in the immediate vicinity of the ministry — unusual, where Taipei was concerned — there were still some within walking distance. When a protest did take place near a convenience store, it never seemed to occur to the riot police that it would have a more difficult time digging in its heels if they acted to block off access. In many ways I was quite suited to the kind of protests that went on through the night and into the dawn. I was good at keeping myself awake, fueled by adrenaline. I had always been something of an insomniac, and it was easy to keep going for a long time, especially if I was also fueled by caffeine.

I finally started to tire when the sun began to peel back the darkness and it became even hotter. As morning approached, it was clear that the occupation was primarily being led by a group of high schoolers, though I couldn't tell whether this was a group that already existed or if they had just emerged spontaneously in the course of the night. Around 8am, they demanded a meeting with the Minister of Education. The press began putting out their spin pieces around that time as well, as usual blaming the students for being socially disruptive and impeding the orderly functioning of government — something that struck me as a claim that might have come directly from the government itself. An inside source within the Ministry of Education had informed me that there were underground tunnels beneath the government buildings in the Shandao Temple area that dated from the Japanese colonial period. Despite the occupation, ministry employees were still able to get to work.

At 10am, Monica, a friend of mine and Ray's, came and brought breakfast for us. She had been unable to make it herself but had been in touch with us through the night. I appreciated the gesture. One of the snacks she brought us was a box of Want Want crackers, which she mostly meant as a joke.

"Taiwan needs you two!" she had said, telling us to take care of ourselves. Well, I liked that thought, but I wondered if it was true.

I had been providing updates on our Facebook page and Twitter through the night — it was a lot of sifting through conflicting sources of information about something occurring in real time around me, trying to maintain my concentration as best I could. As we sat in the parking lot and chatted, I managed to dash off an article with the aid of a can of Red Bull that Monica had brought. The piece began with the words, "Probably yesterday will go down as a day of great heroism and tragedy for Taiwan."

Some old pro-independence types had started to stream in during the morning hours. At night, it had mostly been young people there. By this point, many were already asleep. The dynamic of an occupation changes a lot by the morning. You're tired and the riot police are tired, too, and it's less easy for the police to uproot an occupation by dawn. The daily news cycle has started, so violent acts are more likely to be reported on — and people filter in then, too, having heard the news. Often, it's the struggle to last until dawn that's important if you want a successful occupation, sticking together until daybreak.

I checked for messages from Xixi and kept my responses intentionally vague when she asked what I was doing. News spreads, after all. It seemed unlikely that they wouldn't already have known about this in China, but I wasn't completely sure, and the idea that I might be leaking information put me on edge, especially as we were all drained. Ray said she would take a twenty-minute nap and fell asleep resting on one of the pillars of the ministry building.

I spotted a Taiwanese artist I knew from New York and had a brief chat with him. He had stayed out for the entirety of the night, too, though I hadn't noticed him. I also spotted Dr Tsay, the leader of the Referendum Alliance. I waved.

We left around noon. Ray drove me back, blaring the soundtrack to *Days of Being Wild* in her Prius. She was always listening to the soundtracks to Wong Kar-wai movies whenever she drove around.

"I'm going to sleep for a few hours and head back," I said when I got out. She didn't say anything but nodded wearily, and I surprised myself when I did, in fact, manage to get up by late afternoon.

That night we had an impromptu meeting among *Daybreak* members at the occupation. Originally, the plan was to have a more formal meeting for members who were out of Taiwan at the moment or who lived overseas to join, but we discovered that quite a few people were planning on heading to the occupation that night anyway, so we met around 10pm, buying some snacks and drinks from one of the 7/11s in the area and sitting off to the side of Zhongshan South Road.

The night seems endless sometimes. At the occupation, the smell of sweat and gasoline from the generators was thick. When I look back at my youth, I know that's what I'll remember the most.

It felt a bit like being at a night market or somewhere like that, charged with a sense that this was the place to be — that this was where all the world was. That was probably part of what attracted me to occupations: the feeling that this was the locus of history at that moment, the lever upon which I could move the world. Those were the only times I felt like I was solid, cohering, something more than just a ghost riding around in my own body, observing events as they happened to it.

"This is our chance!" I remember saying. "I always regretted that *Daybreak* didn't exist during the Sunflower Movement.

We missed that opportunity. But this is our time. This is why *Daybreak* exists, isn't it? If we don't do this, who will?"

A grand pronouncement, met by silence. The rest of the team seemed less convinced. What followed was an argument, though not an especially tense one, and I quickly became frustrated at our inability to formulate any concrete plans for how to strategically intervene in the movement. I felt that our response to the previous night's events had been too slow, but we were an entirely volunteer-run publication with zero resources, and all of us were activists, so very often *Daybreak* was just one of many things we were involved in.

The meeting took place as we ate, drank, and smoked. In the end, I drank the entirety of a small bottle of whiskey that Ray had bought and became belligerent. The rest of the night is a blank. I woke up the next morning sleeping in a bush, alone. I guess I had become so unbearable that the others had just left me behind. But drinking too much and blanking out... well... it wasn't exactly uncommon for me. The rest of the team had long since become used to it. Honestly, I think back to my drunken rages and I suppose they just put up with me because of my abilities in other areas.

I checked my phone. There was a text from Ray. "You alive?" I was, for better or worse. She had called me several times during the early morning hours, but I had been passed out.

"I'm alive. But I'm drained," I texted her.

"You can sleep when you're dead," she said. I sighed and picked myself up off of the ground. Us *Daybreak* folks were all broken in our own ways, I knew, but perhaps, for some reason I still couldn't understand, I was more broken than most.

Things picked up after that in terms of mobilizing the team to try to take action. We tended to be bad at formulating plans. Things just happened. Not so different from any social movement group, maybe.

By the afternoon of the first day, a small tent city had sprung up in the parking lot of the Ministry of Education. I found it uncannily reminiscent of the one that existed around the Legislative Yuan during the Sunflower Movement, down to the way the occupation was set up with a phalanx of riot police blocking the front entrance of the building and another one blocking the side entrance.

Repetition but also difference. What was quite striking was how the leadership of the occupation was so much younger than we had been even just a year ago. I liked that, the sense that younger people were picking up the struggle now. I looked forward to when we would be irrelevant. We all just wanted to get at something concrete, I suppose.

Much as had happened during the Sunflower Movement, numerous works of art sprang up in the occupation encampment. There were caricatures of the minister of education, prints with a variety of slogans on them pasted to the side of the building. Wild lilies had been strewn along the razor wire. Engraved in my memory is what someone had written on a building pillar in red paint: "Brainwashing kills."

Some of the indie bands popular in Taiwan came and played during the nighttime, and I heard Sorry Youth play for the third time. Freddy Lim of the New Power Party — a heavy metal musician turned politician — came and gave a speech. Indie DaDee, the rock festival organizer, came and did a 大腸花論壇, a protest staple since last year's movement which largely consisted of members of the public being invited to drink Taiwan Beer and curse the government. The humid summer heat, the music, the people thronging with desire for their own future coursing through their veins, the smell of smoke, sweat, and gasoline: that's what it meant to be young. We *were* alive, weren't we? I tried to lose myself in it all, but I still had a nagging sense of worry where Xixi was concerned that I couldn't shake off.

The high school students tried to negotiate a few times with the government but were unsuccessful in establishing dialogue. I interviewed one of the leaders for a film segment during one of the failed attempts at dialogue, and I was impressed with how cogent he was. When negotiations were finally held with the Ministry of Education, they took place in the National Central Library, though they broke down relatively quickly, with the students storming out of the meeting room in tears when the minister refused to back down. They didn't seem like real tears — it looked to me more like a show for the media than anything else. Yet I was struck once again by how young they all were.

A moment during the meeting when the Minister couldn't help but roll his eyes at the students was picked up and made into a .gif, which was circulated on the Internet endlessly afterwards. It made people angry. As for me, I found it incredible how quickly the high schoolers were able to exploit the gaffe, to make it into something that was reproducible and easily distributed on social media. It attested to their creativity. The kids were alright, I thought.

Perhaps Ryo Lin's suicide had pushed those who were even younger to action. Did that give his life — and death — meaning, I wondered. We churned out articles and news updates all the while. There were a few times when it looked like police might come in and clear the occupation, especially when the numbers of people thinned out overnight.

At one point, it was discovered that a water truck registered to the central government — and not the city government — was parked behind the Ministry of Education. The Taipei mayor, Ko, who had been elected in the wake of the Sunflower Movement the previous year, had stated that he would do his best to prevent the student demonstrators from being violently evicted. But a water truck belonging to the central government wouldn't have to take orders from Ko and could circumvent him.

I drank a lot that week. Alcohol and writing had always gone hand in hand for me, and I was doing the lion's share of my writing at night, while drinking. There were a few nights I woke up in the morning with a hangover and no real memory of how I got into bed, but with a completed or half-completed article on my laptop. What does Baudelaire say about alcohol again? That you should always be drunk? But getting blackout drunk by yourself is kind of sad, no two ways about it.

It was always the same clerk at the Family Mart whenever I showed up to buy my nightly bottle of whiskey and usually a small carton of instant noodles. I often wondered what he thought of my lifestyle. But more than likely, he didn't judge me. Those days, I went to sleep every day around 6 or 7am and woke up around noon. I usually went for oyster noodles or potstickers when I woke up; good food for hangovers. I would grab coffee from the 7/11 a little down the street from my apartment. Then, when I felt sobered up, I would go back to the Ministry of Education to get a sense of the situation on the ground. I would do some writing there, take photos, and walk to one of the coffee shops by Taipei Main Station if I needed to use Wi-Fi to upload photos or articles. At night, I would go back and watch the performances by bands, if there were any, or otherwise just shoot the breeze with whoever was passing through.

I was ostensibly a student then, back in Taipei for classes in the midst of graduate school — not that I went to class often. But during the occupation I skipped classes entirely. The rest of the *Daybreak* crew worked or had other commitments, but nonetheless, sometimes they would join me at night and we'd sit off to the side of the occupation with snacks and Taiwan Beer from yet another convenience store. We might buy some "democracy sausage" from people who would show up nightly on motorcycles and set up little stands to roast and sell them, a protest tradition in Taiwan that had started at some point during the democracy movements of decades past. The sausages were quite tasty, though a bit pricey.

Ray and I were the people who were there most consistently. We had a reputation for being diehards, I suspect. I guess it helped that we were between things, in many respects. That gave us time for activism that we would've lacked if we'd had full-time jobs. But a sense of placelessness, of being adrift, was another motivator. Perhaps occupations are full of people between things — I suspected that was why there had been so many student movements throughout history: it was a period in life between states, roles, responsibilities. Was it just another name for *the emptiness*? But how long could or should that inbetweenness be maintained?

"Until you die like a dog," *the emptiness* said to me.

The occupation had broken out in opposition to the changes to Taiwanese history textbooks for high schoolers that the KMT hoped to pass, an attempt not only to whitewash its own authoritarian past, but to promote positive views of China too. After all, the KMT hoped for political unification between Taiwan and China. And downplaying what took place there, in terms of crackdowns on political freedoms, human rights defenders, and whatever the hell else, was part and parcel of that.

Over the past few years there had been cases of media outlets being bought up by various captains of industry who hoped to use them as another avenue for advancing positive views of China.

And yet here I was dating a Chinese person, despite professing to support Taiwanese independence. I didn't think that was a contradiction though. Wasn't Su Beng — the Marxist revolutionary and so-called grandfather of Taiwanese independence — married to a Japanese woman, and not too long after the Japanese colonial period? But I suspected that part of the reason why I loved Xixi was because of what she represented rather than who she was. Maybe I felt some kind of attachment to China, or perhaps it was all to convince myself that I hadn't in fact become some Taiwanese nationalist, in spite of my background.

Another part of me knew that I couldn't be with a Chinese person forever, since one day there would be repercussions — unless they themselves were willing to pay a high price to be with me. There were times I would come under attack from the "Fifty Cent Party": hired Internet trolls paid by the Chinese government to target and harass voices critical of China on the Internet. They would find me on Twitter or Facebook and leave harassing posts, threatening to hack me and release my personal information or things of that sort. None of them had followed up on those kinds of threats, and I wasn't important enough to affect Xixi yet. But who knew what would happen? Internet trolls would only be the start of it. The real danger was that the Chinese government would take action against her as a way of getting at me. The list of things they could do was endless. Arbitrary detention, harassment, threats, any number of possibilities. If I continued with my life the way it was, it would happen someday, and that increased danger would carry with it the paradoxical satisfaction of knowing I had accomplished something.

As she was on my mind, I decided to call her. At that point we were using Skype.

"How's the visa coming along?" I asked.

"I sent it off, but no answer yet."

"I see," I said. "I sure hope it's not because of me."

"I'm sure it's not. You're not that important." She laughed. Honestly, I wasn't. I just wanted to be.

I sighed. "Sorry, I can't help but worry."

"You're too much of a worrier, Ah-Qiu," she said. "You worry about everything. And anything."

"I guess that's true."

I had met Xixi because after having somehow drifted into graduate school following the Sunflower Movement, I had made friends with a lot of the Chinese students. But academic life felt so unremarkable. Academia was an elephant's graveyard, I caught myself thinking sometimes: a place where half-dead dead things went to die. I just hadn't been able to come up with anything else to do. She was a master's student like me, also studying Chinese literature — a shy, quiet girl who seemed to have very few friends or hobbies. She spent most of her time just watching movies or reading books in her apartment. She often joked that she was a 宅女. Well, it was true. She was always staring at the ground. Her most distinctive feature was probably her red hair, though after a while she stopped dying it and it all faded to black.

We met at some Chinese student function pretty early on in grad school. That day, Xixi had just been off in a corner on her own, and I had started talking to her. Things just went from there, step by step. She was a few years older than me, and she seemed to be in the US to get away from her parents and the pressure to marry and have kids and all that. Those were also the years that "leftover women" were something that was widely discussed among those of us in English-language academia in China. I guess she was that too — a Chinese woman who was unmarried in her late twenties.

She was from Wuhan — in the years before anyone had ever heard of that place. I asked her what the local "dialect" — if you wanted to call it that rather than "language" — sounded like once. I didn't understand a word. We talked in Mandarin as we shared no other mutual language besides English, and her English wasn't the most fluent. She had a strong Beijing accent, though she wasn't from Beijing either. Despite my own accent being somewhat off, I was surprised that the first time we talked, she asked me if I was Taiwanese after a few minutes. Something about my vocabulary maybe.

There was something wistful that I really liked about her; maybe because I, in contrast, was all too aware of the anger that had built up in me over the years. All relationships are built on some kind of projection, and there was a part of me that wanted to get away from the person I had become through my relationship with her.

At the end of the day, perhaps I wasn't satisfied being some kind of activist-journalist forever. I wanted to leave something behind, something that existed beyond me. In those days, I sat in the library daily, even if I didn't really have anything specific to do there. I could read the entire work of most human beings in a day, and it made me despair — consuming all these words and knowing my own life's work wouldn't even amount to a single day's worth of reading.

When it got dark out, I would head home and eat dinner with Xixi in her apartment, which was on the way back to mine walking from the Columbia campus. I did that most days, and usually she cooked. Being pretty useless in the kitchen, I would just help her out with menial tasks while offering color commentary. She couldn't stand this about me, and was always making comments about not understanding how I had survived before I met her. I knew this was quite revealing about me.

When she was in college, she had been a contestant on one of the televised singing contests in China, and had gotten as far as being a finalist. When I asked her why she had ended up participating in the contest, she said her parents, who were music teachers, had talked her into it. She enjoyed singing, and she was good at it, but, of course, she also had the nagging sense that she had no talent of her own, that she was coasting off her parents'.

Still, I would watch the videos once in a while on Youku. She looked pretty in them — I really liked that; or rather, I liked seeing her be so confident. Xixi had an unassuming personality, so it was uncharacteristic of her. I couldn't help but think that had been the high point of her life — that nothing after would ever reach that peak again — and I felt the same way about myself now. The Sunflower Movement and the historical moment that had come with it had passed. I felt it had been a time that summed up and encapsulated my past, present, and future. The rest was just a post-script. My own peak had passed too, had it not?

I only saw her perform once, for a Lunar New Year event organized by some Chinese association in New York. It was just her on stage — no band — with a backing track. I knew it was quite a few steps down compared to when she performed with a whole band on a stage with tens of thousands of viewers watching on television. And yet that was maybe the one and only time I saw her fully in her element.

"Well," she said, "I have to get going. Class." This snapped me out of my reverie.

"Say hi to your students for me," I said.

"Watch out for the typhoon," she quipped and smiled.

I had a lot of long conversations with Xixi late at night that week, partly due to the fact that I was stressed and needed to talk to someone who had no connection to the events I was caught up in. I had long since known, going back to my experiences with Occupy, that when you're completely caught up in a social movement, you lose sight of the world at large — it leads to a sort of tunnel vision.

I enjoyed chatting with her about literature, and it was comforting talking about something that wasn't directly relevant to my immediate experience — except that works of literature, when you traced them back long enough, revealed the connections and repetitions that had all led up to the present moment. One author we could never agree on was Pai Hsien-yung. I hated *Taipei People* the most out of all his books.

"You just don't like it because it reminds you of yourself. And your parents."

I laughed. I couldn't deny that. There were other parallels, probably, since it all seemed to be about people who had similar backgrounds to me as waishengren, and who seemed to have nothing else in life besides their longing for the lost totality of China.

"Come on," she had said to me when I said all this. "Don't you think he also is criticizing them in some ways?" I suggested that perhaps we could ask him ourselves — he was still alive, in his late seventies. Another one of Pai's books was *New Yorkers*. New York and Taipei. The nexus of the two cities evidenced a particular sort of background, which was mine too. *New Yorkers* was even based on Pai's own experiences as a graduate student in New York.

I was undecided on what my thesis topic would be at the time, but was unable to decide between writing on Lu Xun or Wu Chuo-liu.

"It's ironic you can't decide between a Chinese and Taiwanese author," Xixi had said. On the one hand, there was already a lot of work on Lu Xun, on the other there was very little on Wu in English, but that would mean the thesis would perhaps suffer from being attached to a name with little recognition. As for her, she was dead set on writing on Zhuangzi and Daoist thought as it came up in *The Dream of the Red Chamber*. She had an abiding interest in Daoism. I in turn thought it was somewhat ironic to end up with someone with such a strong interest in Daoism in light of how much I had fought with David about it in the years before. But that had been based on what I saw as his Western fantasy of traditional Chinese philosophy — rather different to Xixi's situation and her background as a Chinese person.

The consolations of literature were many, but still it was never enough. She was happy just writing on writing, producing text on texts. I was surprised that, unlike me, she had no interest in writing anything herself. We were each drawn to the other out of loneliness, probably; a shared but differently countered *emptiness*. And yet, I think there was some kind of intimacy there. That is, I don't think we ever had any feeling of being particularly passionate about each other, but it was comfortable being with Xixi, and I was happy, at least briefly. In the end, I think that I missed the only possibility I might have had for a normal life.

Ray was having her own relationship woes that week. Since we were the two members of *Daybreak* consistently at the occupation, night after night, I heard a lot about her most recent ex over alcohol and cigarettes.

"She's moving back to Taipei," Ray said, smoking a cigarette. We were already through a few cans of Taiwan Beer. "I don't know how I'll stand it, living in the same city as her."

"Taipei is a big place," I said. "Doesn't mean you'll run into her."

"But we have a lot of mutual friends."

"That's true." She had a point. I was one of those mutual friends, after all. It was inevitable, and that was one of the brutal things about Taipei. "You ever read Proust, by the way?"

"No."

"I've read *In Search of Lost Time*. I read it all when I was twenty so I could say that I read Proust before I was twenty-one."

"I'm sure that's a good thing to say to impress women at cocktail parties."

"Hey!" I laughed. "What cocktail parties do you think I'm going to exactly?" I took a puff of my cigarette, which I had borrowed from her. Sometimes I smoked just to fit in with certain crowds. With Ray, probably it was just to have something to puff on in the middle of conversation.

"Anyway — Proust comments on how people associate relationships with places and periods of time. I think that may be true of how you feel. People. Associations. Feelings. All of that stuff gets tied together with your memories of yourself in a certain time and place and it all ends up compressed together."

"I know a lot of it is in my imagination. You think about it anyway though, right?" She took a long drag of her cigarette. "You never really know other people to begin with. You just imagine you do."

"You only know your subjective view of that person," I said. "You never actually know them. That's a sad thing, isn't it? It sort of points to how it's impossible to really know people."

"Human, all too human. But she felt like... the one?"

"You got that right. Anyway, rationally, I don't believe in destiny or anything like that. Soulmates. Whatever. But I know how you feel."

"I'm just a romantic at heart," said Ray. I was being mocked, I knew. I had a tendency to say that often too.

"It's hard not to be." I sighed. "Say, can I borrow another cigarette?" I had thought I'd quit after the Sunflower Movement, but it was harder to really stop smoking than I had hoped.

Ray sighed. "Sometimes... I just want to disappear."

"Who doesn't, sometimes?" I said. "Why do you love her?" My question was met with silence.

"Because she completes me…?" Ray laughed at the cliché, and so did I. She didn't have an answer either.

I didn't really know what it was like to have a rich emotional life with ups and downs, so I always tried to take Ray seriously. Maybe a part of me envied her sense of lived experience, emotional investiture. Any emotional turmoil I just kept to myself if I could.

She took another pull on her cigarette. Ray was always going out of her way to try to come off as Bohemian and cool. She had always watched the latest movie or read the latest book and was always hanging out at some hip bar or cafe. How seriously could I take what she was saying? Was it all just some aesthetic pose? Was that how people saw me, as well? I would never really know. A part of me had the sense that we would all look back at this later — say, ten years on — and laugh. That's part of growing up, too. Still, I couldn't stand the idea that it was just as those who criticized us said: that we were just another generation of angry youths who would grow up one day and become the same as the adults we despised.

I was also thinking back to when I was hanging out with David and Aoi in coffee shops. In retrospect, a lot of our conversations felt frivolous, yet I still thought back to those times often. Maybe I was just feeling nostalgic. Or maybe a part of me was drawn to the sense of what was familiar but different. After all, nothing ever stood still.

"You mean that we'll change?"

I nodded.

"I don't know. Some things can't be changed."

"It's called growing old. We won't be in our twenties forever."

"There are some things you don't want to take back either, right?"

And it was true. It had already been a few years since I had talked to Neil. Some things there's no going back from. There were people I would never talk to again, as long as I lived — and I knew it was less about the person themselves and more about what they had come to represent for me. Because it would make me face a part of myself which I really didn't feel like I wanted to.

The occupation couldn't last forever. We knew it. So did the students. Exhaustion sets in eventually, and everything falls apart because people just can't go on anymore. Life is like that, too, come to think of it. And relationships. Things can get messy when it all falls apart. People get tired of causes they would have otherwise supported when an occupation goes on too long. The tail end of the Umbrella Movement the year before was like that. The public grew weary of an occupation taking up so much space in the city center.

Besides, there was also the typhoon that was approaching Taiwan. It was said to be the largest storm in the world that year, and I admit, there was something about the thought of high schoolers facing off against the wrath of nature that I found romantic. Some of the threats they faced were man-made too. The Grey Wolf had publicly declared that he would be coming to the occupation on the night of 6 August.

Earlier that week, he and his pack of gangsters had demonstrated outside of the DPP's headquarters dressed as Japanese imperial soldiers. The claim was that the DPP was behind the protests, hence the protest there. It was the usual kind of claim that one saw from authoritarians — they never seemed to believe that any kind of spontaneous protest could truly be *spontaneous* and were always convinced there had to be some kind of external force propping it up.

The Grey Wolf's appearance in Japanese imperial costume was all a bit ridiculous, like some strange act of cosplay. It was hard to wrap your head around, but it all had to do with how Chinese nationalists such as the Grey Wolf were always accusing pro-independence groups of being Han traitors who fawned over the Japanese. It was true that pro-independence groups were sometimes nostalgic for the Japanese colonial era, seeing the Japanese's treatment of Taiwanese during the colonial period as better than the KMT's. But even odder for me was to be reminded how, in some strange way, people like that were kin to me. Was I any different? After all, I also craved power, didn't I?

It was another scorching summer night and there was a lot of unease at the occupation. Students arrayed themselves outside of the Ministry of Education in rows. Shortly after 7pm, the Taiwan Solidarity Union, a pro-independence third party, made a surprise appearance. They were carrying placards with slogans about defending the students. Would it actually help? I had as little idea as anyone. I honestly didn't like them — they were pro-independence, but conservative on social issues.

We spotted riot police off to the side of the road, clad in black riot gear. What did this mean? Obviously, they weren't on our side. But the KMT had to make certain gestures to democratic politics, too, if it wanted to come off as not just a resurgent authoritarian party.

And then we were waiting, impatiently waiting, to see if the Grey Wolf would really come; anxiously waiting, since we didn't know what the night would bring.

The students shuffled back and forth among themselves. We all asked the same question of ourselves: Would we see blood that night? The Grey Wolf was, after all, a killer. What level of violence could we expect in post-authoritarian Taiwan?

We all remembered the Umbrella Movement half a year ago and the images of police violence. We ourselves had seen it a year ago, too, during the attempted Executive Yuan occupation. And it's not like we could expect the police to do anything — the police had a long history of working together with gangsters during the authoritarian movement. It's like that everywhere in the world, really. I thought about the cop who had been responsible for all those beatings during 324 — the city was plastered with stickers of him at this point. "HAVE YOU SEEN HIM?" they screamed, since he was never officially reprimanded or named by the police.

I was chatting with a group of foreign journalists we had run into — we were, after all, the main independent English-language outlet to have emerged after the Sunflower Movement — when I realized that the Grey Wolf and his gang were already there on the other side of the road. It was all quite sudden. I wondered how they had gotten here. Was it as mundane as their having taken the subway or boarded a bus? I couldn't remember how they had arrived at the Sunflower Movement the year before, either; it had seemed then as though I blinked and they appeared, teleported into place or risen up from some trapdoor in the stage.

"I'm going to take photos!" I shouted and dashed over. I climbed over a bush in the shrubbery dividing Zhongshan South Road and slipped past the riot police standing at attention and into the thick of the Grey Wolf's supporters. A lot of them were surprisingly young. They didn't look like gangsters either. I couldn't tell if that meant that the Grey Wolf had genuine supporters, or if they were paid protesters, as they were often rumored to be. Yet it wasn't unthinkable to me that there could simply be a cosmos of young people in Taiwan that I had very little idea about. We were all locked into our various echo chambers, weren't we?

They carried signs with anti-Japanese slogans, and a stage had been set up on which they were giving speeches. How long had that taken? In the totality of the occupation, many things escape your attention. I got up close to the stage, slipping through the crowd. It never took me too much time to work my way through crowds. I guess I was just used to dealing with protests. And there he was, the Grey Wolf, within arm's reach. I started snapping away, while mentally making a note of what he was saying. A part of me was already drafting the article in my head. How to frame this all. How to describe it. What kind of angle I would take.

It was only then that I realized this could be dangerous. I was always being mistaken for Japanese, for some reason — probably it had to do with the fact that I had Asian features but my body language was slightly different from everyone else's — and, well, I was in the thick of anti-Japanese nationalists with organized crime ties. There might have been gangsters among them willing to use violence — *to kill*. What was there to prevent me from getting beaten to death? It was hard to imagine in post-authoritarian Taiwan — but not *unthinkable*.

I was close enough to the Grey Wolf that I could have tried to drag him off the stage if I'd wanted. It was strange: I always seemed to be at the bottom of the stage, looking up at some man — usually at some protest leader. It was tempting, somehow; the thought of pulling him down. Maybe I always resented those who were on the stage. But then doing something like that really would have meant death, and the thought came into my head: What if I just *killed* the Grey Wolf, then and there? I was standing in front of the stage he was standing on. I didn't think it would be impossible for me to grab his ankles, pull him off, and snap his neck. I didn't have a black belt for nothing, not that it had ever been useful.

Was it really that easy to kill someone? You hit someone on the wrong part of their head and they can die. It makes you realize how fragile the human body really is. I would probably get torn to shreds by the Grey Wolf's supporters in the next moment, but maybe it wouldn't be a bad way to go. Maybe it would make all of it, life, worth it, and I was faced again with the question of whether I was willing to lay my life down for a cause. In their final photographs, you can see that many of those executed during the White Terror went to their deaths with a smile, wanting to be remembered that way, as unbroken and so deeply oriented to something beyond themselves that death itself died in the face of their commitment. This is the path to a good death, a happy death, they seemed to say. Those images bubbled up to the surface of my consciousness. In a revolution, you might have only a moment to decide if it's worth dying for something. A moment to decide the weight of your life. Perhaps that moment was here.

My grandfather had come to Taiwan as a military official with Chiang and the KMT. Like Chiang, he was from Zhejiang, which was probably why he was trusted as one of Chiang's direct associates — Chiang trusted people from the same province most of all. He wasn't so different from the Grey Wolf, was he? The Grey Wolf was the right age. He could have potentially been my father.

I knew that my grandfather had been part of the Taiwan Garrison Command and that he'd had a direct role in the killings during the White Terror. He never talked about the details, but he had never expressed regret over it either. As he put it, those were merely the actions of a different era. How comfortable for him to be able to die in democratic Taiwan, without having ever had been called to account for his actions. I was the one who could redeem this bloody history — that of my own origin — was I not? Who could reclaim the history that should have been — even if it was by means of my own death.

Maybe I had a different sense of right and wrong. But I wondered: Had he thought about whether he was willing to die for the nation he believed in? Probably he had — he was willing to go to jail for years for it, after all. And he was willing to kill for it. If the moment came, would I have such conviction? Was I truly a leftist? Or was I also just a nationalist? Maybe just a Taiwanese nationalist and not a Chinese one. Wasn't that the fascist dream too? To give one's life up for a cause beyond yourself. To be just another human bullet? Some really relished that. As for me, I thought there was a time to kill one's father, one's grandfather, to smash all memorial tablets and bury the past. To finally lay the monster that is history to rest.

I would kill the Grey Wolf and die. I would revenge myself upon my own past and all those who had suffered under us. It would be a fratricide, heroic, poetic even. The journalist the Grey Wolf had killed in California was Taiwanese American by naturalization. Some decades later, if the Grey Wolf was killed by a journalist who was Taiwanese American by birth, it would seem like poetic justice. I wondered how the headlines would read: "Taiwanese American Journalist Kills Killer of Taiwanese American Journalist and Is Then Killed"? I was always thinking about interesting ways to die. If I wasn't caught up in something, life seemed boring. Dying in a strange and interesting way might be a good way to end it all. That would be a satisfying way to fulfill the arc of my life, wouldn't it, V?

All too often, life seemed a long, interminable slog. A slow march to oblivion, only punctuated by occasional moments of excitement. And I was getting bored. Human, all too human — all too *boring* sounds more to the point. Besides, for several years now, the decay in my body, *the emptiness*, had been gnawing away at me. I knew I didn't have a lot of time until it ate me alive. Better end it all before I became someone other than myself. And better end it all before *the emptiness* consumed not only me but the world.

"Choose your death!" *the emptiness* said to me.

And then I snapped back to the here and now as the reality principle reasserted itself. I found that I was sweating, and not just because of how hot the night was. It had only been a moment — a fleeting impulse, but it felt as though it had lasted a lifetime. My thoughts were again on the article, on the words that would go onto a page about these experiences; words about the thing in place of the thing itself.

I found that I was taking photographs mechanically and without paying much attention, and deciding that I had taken enough, I went back and found my friends again. Bands had started playing over the intercom system to drown out the noise of the Grey Wolf and his rally.

A shout and a cry. The riot police started closing off the rally, coming in with their batons and riot gear. I was surprised to see them come in, frankly. But even for them, the optics of just doing nothing when literal gangsters turned up may have been too much. It could have been that the police didn't take kindly to having their authority infringed upon by the Grey Wolf and company; outrage over police inaction the year before was probably another contributing factor.

"Come on!" said Ray. "We should get out of here." We started running and barely got out before they closed off the barrier.

I remember being impressed by how many people had gathered at the occupation after hearing that the Grey Wolf would be coming. That was the biggest crowd I saw gathered at the Ministry of Education during the occupation. A lot of people had been motivated to come out by the possibility of violence being used against the student occupiers. The atmosphere had been comradely, festive. Somebody tried organizing people to link arms, as if that might act as a deterrent. There was something in that, in what it meant to stand with a group, which acted as a counterbalance to my earlier impulses regarding the fantasy of dying alone, nobly, for some cause — self-destruction as aesthetic pleasure, perhaps, rather than erasing everything.

The gaps in your own self could only be filled through collective action with others, solidarity of the present as counterposed to the darkness of the past. I tried to focus on that feeling, the feeling of togetherness, to drown out that other feeling — that I was still there, an arm's length of the Grey Wolf.

In the end, little else occurred besides both sides shouting at each other, and it was a bit of a pitiful end for the Grey Wolf's rally, really. Maybe that was just how this kind of thing went down in Taiwan's democratic era. It had been more dangerous in preceding eras, in the age when political killings were still commonplace. In addition, in contemporary times it was harder to carry out acts of violence and get away with it — everyone who had a smartphone could potentially take photos or record, and there were security cameras across the city.

Perhaps what had taken place was just the last gasp of the past.

"How long have we been here?" Ray asked. We were standing in the median strip of a road, watching the police clear out people.

"It's been a few hours," I said.

"It's time for dinner," she said. "Jinfeng?"

"Alright." I chuckled. From pondering self-annihilation back to the mundane realities of what to eat in the space of an hour. Jinfeng was a well-known braised pork rice place that wasn't too far off. I liked the food, but it reminded me once again about my background: my family was like one of the KMT families from the neighborhood around Guling Street — the area where Edward Yang's *A Brighter Summer Day* is set. In the post-war years, Taiwan's major gangs — such as the Grey Wolf's — were originally formed by troubled KMT kids from those neighborhoods, who met on basketball courts. In my generation, troubled kids ended up in social movements. Perhaps these are the twin fates of those who are orphaned by society, by the world.

We drove off in Ray's car to find food. As we started to drive away, we spotted Qiu Xiulian rooting through a bush, looking like she was looking for something she had dropped. Qiu was part of a group that was always waving Chinese flags outside Taipei 101, the world's tallest skyscraper at the time of its construction. One of the Grey Wolf's close associates, a few weeks before, she'd made the news for beating a Falun Gong practitioner bloody. Noticing us staring, she awkwardly nodded at us — I found the way in which she did so strangely polite — then continued rooting. Ray and I both stared, then the light changed and we drove off.

That was the strange close of a strange night. It was all a bit anticlimactic. I had missed another chance to die.

Perhaps you are my last chance, V. Perhaps it was always you.

The true end of the occupation was the next day. In some way, the Grey Wolf's visit had given it a last burst of energy. You might even say that he had provided the high point of the occupation.

There were conflicting reports about whether the students were planning on withdrawing or not. Some days before, they had claimed that they would only be withdrawing once their demands about rescinding the planned textbook changes were met, typhoon or no typhoon, but it became obvious that they would be withdrawing once I realized that there were no preparations at the occupation encampment to weather the storm.

Every occupation needs to have an endgame, because rarely do occupation-style movements win all their demands; exhaustion sets in, and there's no longer any way to keep going. There's always a need to end on a high note, to keep the energy of the movement alive in some form, and so they ended with a memorial ceremony for Ryo Lin before announcing they would be withdrawing. The ceremony went on for an hour and a half, the students lighting candles and a line of mourners gathering and bowing in front of his picture. I took some photos, then joined the line of mourners myself.

Probably we would never know the reason why Lin died. The movement against the textbook changes had been stalling in previous months. He may have been hoping to die for a cause, too. The authorities had told him after his arrest that he would have no future, that he would never be able to find work with the taint of an arrest on his record. Maybe their attempt to convince him that he had died a "social death" led to his real death. Apparently, he had been fond of saying that he would not live beyond twenty. It wasn't the first time that someone so young had died: in the authoritarian era, there had been some even younger who had been put to death. Nor was he the first person to die for a cause in the apparent hopes that their death could provoke change. The most famous of all was probably "Nylon" Cheng Nan-jung, the journalist and publisher who had self-immolated after a standoff with police that lasted for seventy-one days. Those were the years in which the KMT cracked down on any magazine or publication that strayed from the official ideology. Cheng had been a leftist advocate of Taiwanese independence, opening dozens of magazines that were then shut down. He chose to end his life in flames when the police finally came for him. I wondered if that would be my fate, too, someday. I was all too clear — a part of me wanted that kind of heroic death and to be remembered that way in the annals of world history.

During the ceremony, some of the students were in tears. I imagine many of them knew Lin. They had stuck it out for the week, with the eyes of the nation upon them. It could only have been an emotional roller coaster. But in the end, they bowed and thanked everyone for their support. That was it. It had started raining during the end of the ceremony, just as the sun went down. As the students set about dismantling the occupation site, I took shelter under the roof of the Ministry of Education building.

Ray called me. She hadn't been able to get off work in time to make it for the withdrawal, but we decided to go to a bar in Xinyi to celebrate. Oddly enough, the rain stopped almost as soon as we got there. So much for the climactic storm.

The bar, which was Ray's favorite, looked classy on the outside, but it seemed to be a mom-and-pop establishment. The family dogs were always camped out in the back. Well, I didn't dislike classy places either, but Xinyi bars made me a bit uncomfortable sometimes. I much preferred the vibe of Brother Tseng's place or Pub.

Xinyi was a strange neighborhood, as the fancy downtown area in Taipei seemed a world away from the isolated government buildings on the other side of town where we had just been. The neighborhood had really developed after Taipei 101 was built. Taipei 101 towered over everything in the neighborhood — no building came close to it in height anywhere in the city, even ten years after it was finished.

We sat at the bar. We were the only people there, given the typhoon. Nobody else from *Daybreak* had been willing to come out. Just us, then.

"Feel satisfied?" I asked Ray. "It's all over."

"We did our best, didn't we?"

"I never know what to do with myself after something like this."

"The post-revolutionary blues."

"That's what it is," I said. "People tell me sometimes that I'm just a thrill seeker, since I'm always doing something like this. Still, what do you think of all this? Did they accomplish anything?"

"Did *we* accomplish anything?"

"It's hard to say. We don't even know yet if the French Revolution was a success, right?" I quipped, referencing a Zhou Enlai quote.

She didn't laugh, but I knew she would get the reference. I had a hard time reading her expression in the semi-darkness, the lights of the city refracting through the rain and onto her face.

"Yeah, it's all so boring really. Life," said Ray. I nodded but didn't say anything. Ray seemed to be thinking about that girl. Sure enough: "I've been thinking lately that if I can't be with her, there's no point for me being around." She lapsed into silence.

"You shouldn't put that much of your self-worth on one person," I said. Like I was anyone to talk.

"What about you?" Ray asked, looking at me for the first time. "How would you feel leaving Xixi behind?"

"Well…" I didn't have an answer.

"As long as I'm alive, I still have a chance, right?" she said, sounding bitter.

"I don't know," I said. "I think humans just cling to chance to keep them sane."

"I thought you didn't believe in destiny."

"I don't. Even so, most of the time, everything is just determined in advance. We perceive things as contingent nonetheless. And maybe there is a small degree of agency that we have in the grand scheme of things, even if we can't determine the facts of our birth or where we find ourselves in life. Pushing against the tide, to change what's already been determined: that's difficult, if not impossible. Is that destiny? I'm not sure."

"If that's so, it doesn't make any difference what we do, think, or feel."

"Most of the time, I don't think it does. But we try to convince ourselves otherwise."

"So, is there meaning to anything?"

"Maybe there's meaning to not dying alone."

That was a lie if I ever heard one. I already knew then that I would be dying alone. It was written in my genes, or maybe the stars. I would just be paying back a blood debt for all the lives I was sure I had taken in past incarnations, for all the lives I had unknowingly taken in this life. A cursed fate, you might call it.

Even dying with you will be dying alone, V.

We walked for a while in the neon lights of Xinyi once the rain had stopped, smoking. Taipei 101 flashed in the distance, towering over the rest of the buildings in the city. It was cool now since the rain had passed.

"You know that line in *Fallen Angels*? About how people can rub up against each other, but it doesn't mean they'll become your lover or confidante? I think it's like that." Ray sighed.

"You're that worried about running into her?"

"Yeah. In my mind, I feel like I'll run into her. So it'll happen."

"But…" I shrugged. "It means that when you're not around, it's all too easy to be forgotten. Humans are just at the mercy of their memories. Or maybe time. You can't win against time."
I was always trying to hold time still. But the thing about the past is that it never comes back. You can only keep on moving forward, no matter how unbearable it is.

"So why bother with anything?" asked Ray. She took a drag of her cigarette, the end glowing red in the darkness.

"If I don't keep moving, I'll fall to pieces. That's all."

"Well, you're alive, aren't you?"

"Me?" I finished off the can of beer I had been drinking, crushed it, and threw it into the streets. It made a hollow sound as it fell to the ground. The rain had stopped. There were no lights. Taipei 101, looming over the city, had gone dark, a monolith against the black night.

Stand at the side of a river long enough and you'll see the corpse of your enemy drifting down. Stand even longer at the side of that river and eventually you'll see yourself drifting down that river, too.

That waiting was *the emptiness,* though I imagine it has many names. After I died for the first time, I had died many times, and every time I died and was reborn, I would wake up, as though from a dream, to find that more and more of me had just rotted away. No matter how many times I died, I never could die the death that I wanted.

I knew I didn't have much time left. It didn't show on the outside, but my insides had been all but eaten away. Looking at my hand, holding it up to the night sky, I could see the maggots. Soon, I wouldn't be able to hold myself together anymore. Then everyone would see that I had been hollowed out long ago. That, for some time, I had been a living corpse.

What was the body but a collection of parts, anyway?

When the maggots had eaten through the seams holding my body together, I would just be a pile of parts. That would be the end. It seemed appropriate even. After all, we never experience the world as a whole, just in fragments and sections. When I was all hollowed out and *the emptiness* had finished consuming me, I would just be the segments of a corpse.

That wasn't the death I had wanted. I had missed my chance to die that death. And I couldn't let *the emptiness* triumph. I had to weave a labyrinth, to trap it within me through words, then die where nobody would ever find my corpse.

Part 4

Before I went back to NYC in the fall of 2015 — right around the end of summer — I spent a week in Tokyo catching up with old friends. Nobody seemed to be doing well. Whenever I went back somewhere, I would always find my friends were just slightly worse off than when I saw them last. Or maybe things were never how I remembered them, never as ideal as I had made them seem the first time I was there.

Xixi broke up with me not too long after I got back to NYC in the fall. I wasn't too surprised. I had already known that it wouldn't be a lasting relationship, so I didn't put up too much of a fight. But still I sat in front of the library daily and read because it was a spot that Xixi passed by often. When she passed, I might have a short and awkward conversation with her; when she realized that was my real reason for being there, she stopped passing by. I continued to sit there daily until it grew too cold and, in that way, I got to know the life patterns and schedules of a number of other people who also took that route — people were so predictable, just like automatons. No doubt I was too.

Sitting in the library, day by day, watching the hours of the day pass by, it was soon winter. There are a lot of people who venture into the archives and just end up as mummies themselves. If you're lucky, you get dug out and put in a museum somewhere. I was constantly in need of more visceral experience: the feeling of running on the streets, of running from tear gas, police batons, and riot shields. Life in New York as a grad student was entirely the opposite. So I dropped out of grad school. It was like the ending of Pai Hsien-yung's *New Yorkers*, after all.

Ray found another girlfriend. They seemed happy together. Maybe she wasn't the person that Ray had been idealizing, but she was happy enough with her. Neil seemed happy, too, in Beijing. I never talked to him again, but that's what I heard through the grapevine. I realized in retrospect that one of the reasons we had fought was because he was uncertain about what he wanted to do with his life.

As for Yuli, she transferred to a different college to try her hand at studying philosophy for a while, then eventually went back to National Yang Ming University. I guess she still had a lot of time to figure out what she wanted to do in life. I felt somewhat envious of her for having the choice.

David is still living in Japan. He never found Aoi. He's still looking. When I look at him, I realize that's something I could never do. I don't know if he'll ever find her. I really doubt it.

I wonder about Aoi sometimes. I'm sure she's still alive out there, somewhere.

Everyone else I just never reconnected with again.

All my friends had settled down. But me? I was still restless.

How far from revolution I was now. Takayama Chogyu says that in the nullity of life, there are three solutions. One is to embrace a lifelong love, another is madness, and the third is death.

So I decided I would die. I hadn't been able to become a deicide, so I would die. That seemed like the most interesting thing to do. And maybe the most selfless.

I would die an undialectical man. Another corpse, just drifting down the river.

It was soon spring. And so, I left New York again and came back to you, V.

Love and revolution are nice things to believe in. But maybe at the end of the day they are just other names for Eros and Thanatos, sex and death. Maybe it's all just an excuse for a long confession, really, or some kind of suicide note.

You see, for me, V, you are *the emptiness*. Your existence is, for me, the existence of *death*. You are the one this all started with, in a time before primordial memory — before there was time itself.

It is a moist summer night, the kind when it's lightly raining. Another night, another time, another place. I cannot tell what city we are in: New York, Tokyo, Taipei. It all blends together. Each city is just a different arrangement of replaceable parts; cities are all permutations of one another.

I am not sure exactly where we are now. There are bright fluorescent lights, like a 7/11, and we are sitting in a row of cheap plastic stools, of the kind you often see in a protest, extending out into infinity. There are shelves behind us, but they are empty. This is a room with no windows, or is it? Is it really night? As far I can see, the landscape outside is just an expanse of blinding white with no horizon. Or is there glass at all? I can make out vast skyscrapers in the distance, blank monoliths towering in the field of white.

I know then; that is where all things have begun and where all things will end; the place *the emptiness* came from, a place without a name. We start life as corpses and end life as corpses — this is the place those corpses come from and return to. The no-place. The center of the corpse-universe.

I think about the past. I think about the present. I think about the future. I think about the people I have met in the course of my life. Everything is just a story within a story within a story. The universe was the corpse of a corpse of a corpse, and we were all just maggots feeding on it.

"Why?" V asks me.

"Because your existence means death for me," I say. "It would have been better if you had just killed me."

"That's how it is?"

"Yeah. That's how it is."

"You're going to die alone."

"I know."

"You like to imagine yourself as the main character of a story, don't you? The tragic hero of some kind of drama?" You shrug. "You really have this strange desire for others to always be watching you. To be looked at. But really, you're not as important as you like to think you are."

"But it's not a dream. This is reality," you continue. "In tribal societies, sometimes they would sacrifice the king, killing him in order to raise him to divinity. The self-abasing narrative has an element of that as well. Which is to say, all forms of self-representation have an element of masturbation. The Christ myth — of the death and resurrection of this kind of king — is itself a form of cannibalism."

"What's the point?" I ask. I am tired. The kind of tiredness when both life and death alike seem like a drunken dream. I make an effort to pull myself together. "I wanted to experience… the purest form of absolute reality," I murmur.

You don't say anything, nor can I read your expression, so I keep going.

"As life has just been one long, protracted process of the world inflicting pain upon me, I used to think the point wasn't to realize a world in which I would no longer feel such pain, but rather to achieve higher, more sublimated, more refined forms of pain. I didn't feel being scarred by the world was any object. On the contrary, I saw myself at the end of time, torn to pieces. I thought if I was reduced to a severed hand lying in the sand, a torso with a beating heart, a thinking Yorick's skull, or a single eye floating in the abyss, it would be fine. But what have I done in life that was not just returning to *the emptiness*?"

A moment, an eyeblink, an eternity, ten thousand years pass. From the first single-celled organism to the last human. It is all just a dance on the grave. In that respect, human consciousness — the ability to become aware of death — is probably a mistake.

"Alright," V says. "I'll kill you. This is your absolute reality."

You take out a knife from your pocket. Grabbing my hair, you jam it into my neck. I don't resist. I crumple right away, backwards into death. "Amor fati," you say. "Vive la mort." You say this like an incantation. "Shall we sing the praises — of death?" you murmur to yourself.

You throw me onto the floor, then lower yourself onto my body. Sitting on top of my chest. you make a horizontal cut starting at my forehead, running from one ear to the other, and pull until my face comes off. You complete the cut at my chin, then throw my face aside.

"Do you know how they describe sacrifices in Zhuangzi?" you ask. "It's not so much cutting apart an animal as releasing its constituent parts from their ties with one another. You have to become one with the ox to cut it to pieces."

Then you reach into my left eye socket and pull, cutting the optic nerve, and throw aside the eye when it comes out of the socket. You do the same for the other eye, reach into my mouth and grab the tongue, then cut it off slowly. It isn't a clean cut. Some amount of tongue is left behind as a bleeding stump. You grab my left ear and twist, sawing it off, and then do the same to my right ear.

Next, you cut open my throat, making a vertical cut that goes down to my chest. You stick your hands into the incision, feeling my throat and vocal cords, then continue to cut down past the navel and all the way to the groin. This you do with practiced movements. You make a horizontal cut. You reach into the chest cavity, as if to pry it open.

You don't need to. The maggots come bubbling out, spilling over my face, crawling into my nose, into my mouth, into my ears, and covering my eyes. The organs in my body have long since been eaten away. I cannot see, hear, or taste anymore. But I can still feel pain. The maggots crawl into my wounds. I feel the rain starting to beat down on me. The maggots keep coming, uncountable in number. They will crawl out of my body and devour the world. *The emptiness* will consume everything.

The only thing that exists is pain. I am a living corpse. But even then, in my pain, I can't help but feel that there is something about this that is so *beautiful*. Dying and death. Withering away. It is ineffably beautiful, decay. This is the nature of the violence that I have been seeking. It fills me with delight. The end of the dream. Time to die, time to wake, the end of the story.

But I didn't die. I'm not dead yet. I missed my chance at death. That doesn't mean I won't die someday. Just that I've put it off for a while.

I wake up and my wounds are gone. I can still feel the maggots crawling inside of me. The next death I die will be the last. You are gone. I can tell you have been gone for a long time, V. Perhaps it has only ever been me.

I've lived a life of continual pain, of continual self-hatred. Death would mean a way out, but I'll continue to live on. I'll continue to inflict more pain on myself. I'll continue to inflict pain on other people. That's the price of living. Maybe that's responsibility.

I'll kill God yet. I'll kill God and snuff out the sun. No more false dawns.

The rain has stopped, but the night isn't over yet. I look out into the dark. She is still out there. I will look for her. The night is the only place where I know myself, after all

The world has an expiration date, which is rapidly approaching. I will continue onward.

Thin bands of monochrome light are creeping through the Taipei skyline now. The start of another day in which to live and die.

At the end of history, I will look back and say: I regret everything; I regret nothing.

ALSO AVAILABLE FROM REPEATER BOOKS

Twelve Cries From Home:

In Search of Sri Lanka's Disappeared

by Minoli Salgado

Since August 2020, the intimidation of witnesses and journalists has surged in Sri Lanka. *Twelve Cries from Home* navigates the memories and stories of twelve war survivors, mostly women and relatives of the disappeared, who wished to have their stories retold so that a permanent record might be made, and so that those outside the country might understand their experiences.

The outcome of a journey across the island in late 2018 by writer and Professor of Literature Minoli Salgado, who was revisiting her ancestral home, this is deeply-layered and localised work of travelling witness. It returns to the concept of home as a place of belonging and security, which is a lost ideal for most, and uses a Sri Lankan measure of distance – the call, or hoowa – to ask how we might attend to stories that are difficult to tell and to hear.

Order online from RepeaterBooks.com

ALSO AVAILABLE FROM REPEATER BOOKS

When The Music's Over:

Intervention, Aid, & Somalia

by Gareth Owen

In this accessible and engaging memoir, Gareth Owen, now Humanitarian Director at Save the Children UK, recounts the entanglement of violence and humanity at the heart of this notorious peacekeeping operation. This is a story of human resilience and contradictory friendships, of loyalty, courage and extraordinary endeavour — but mostly it is a story about the meaning of human connection in desperate circumstances.

Part memoir, part history and part politics, *When the Music's Over* sees beyond the criticism of humanitarian intervention and challenges us to consider the enduring importance of international solidarity in a world where notions of common humanity and universal peace are increasingly being abandoned.

Order online from RepeaterBooks.com